The Missed Call

notionpress
.com

The Missed Call

Purnima Dubey

notionpress.com

Notion Press

Old No. 38, New No. 6
McNichols Road, Chetpet
Chennai - 600 031

First Published by Notion Press 2016

ISBN 978-93-86009-92-0

Dedication

"Manju and Satish Dubey, my parents have always acted as friends in my life and its only because of them that I am here publishing my own book today. My best friend Dhwani has made me have faith in myself and encouraged me to go on writing and making this dream come true. Thanks to my brothers Ankur and Jatin, and my friend Sujay for seeing to it that I do not lack any sort of entertainment in my life. Special thanks to my niece Mishika for being a little bundle of joy and making me instantly happy with her hugs.

Lastly, thank you to my Notion Press team, Shivakumar, Shiny and Charmine for being supportive at all times. My Rise For India family who gave me a chance to explore my skills, my girl gang, my cousins, my wattpad family and all those friends who have always been around, thank you to all of you guys."

CONTENTS

1 PAST

17...17 isn't a very huge number but neither very small. At 17 normal people think about future prospects, they think about girlfriend's and boyfriend's the college they want to get into, what is currently new in trend, latest fashion updates etc etc, but not me. I was left upon with a larger responsibility, I had a small family whom I thought would support me when needed but they ended up leaving when their presence mattered the most. In reality family is a group of close knit people that stay together, not necessarily those bound to us by blood. The people or that person you have around when terror strikes is your family.

I am Rhea, Rhea Sharma; I lost my parents Parul and Aniket Sharma two years ago when I was merely 17 years old. The only person that keeps me alive happens to be my younger sister Sia. Sia was just 14 when one day the police called up on my phone to inform about my parents tragic accident. The memories of that day are still fresh in my mind. They were off to matheran (a small hill station in Maharashtra, India) for their 18th wedding anniversary; I still remember them forcing us to accompany them.

"Rehu beta you too join us, stop changing Sia's decision" said dad, they were well aware that I wasn't letting Sia accompany them, afterall it was their anniversary and we were old enough to be alone for a few days or that's what I thought.

"Mom can you please tell dad we can survive a few days without his constant paternal guidance" mum starts laughing and gives me an assuring smile.

"Aniket let the girls live, they will have the caretaker to take care of them so take a chill pill" dad, me and Sia started laughing sensing mum try to act all cool whereas we all knew she would be the one who would call us every other hour to update on us.

They left early next morning and never came back...

Death is said to take away the soul of a person, but in our case even the bodies were gone. We never got to see them, apparently their car fell in the valley and so the bodies couldn't be found. It seemed very illogical and so I demanded to be taken to the accident spot, as I wasn't an adult I couldn't go alone so I was accompanied by my maternal aunt Rakul, she is mum's elder sister and stays in Gujarat but the moment she heard about the accident she flew down to be with us as she knew the paternal side of my family wouldn't be as grateful.

Reaching there we found that right beside the valley was a river and the police suspected that the bodies could have washed away due to the constantly flowing river. He said a lot more things but I couldn't hear any further words as I was shocked, Rakul aunt kept sobbing and nodding her head at the questions directed towards her. We came back the next day and completed all the rituals, Sia would wake up in the middle of the night and start crying. Everyone cried, but I couldn't, at least not in front of anyone, people used to talk about me being cold hearted and not affected. How was I supposed to react to an accident that left behind nothing to cry over? It is always easier to shed tears but I was choosing the painful way of dealing with things.

5 days later...

"Rhea dear what have you decided"

"About what masi (maternal aunt in Hindi)??"

"You can't live alone for another year you both either have to come with me or your grandma, take your time to decide"

"Ok, I will ask Sia too and will let you know by tomorrow"

"Fine beta, don't stress I know you are very brave and are old enough to decide for yourself"

Passing on a smile to her I lie down on my bed and think about all the harshness that was directed to my little sister and me in the past five days. I knew that somewhere down the line the people that I thought were my family were finding ways to blame us for whatever had happened. I couldn't let my sister live in an environment where she was clearly unwanted. With the final decision made up in my mind I fell asleep.

2 DECISIONS

"*Dear if ever the kids come to know about it what are we supposed to tell them.*"

"*They won't, they never will*"

Again the same dream and the same conversation, ever since mum and dad have left their conversation kept replaying in my mind, my parents were the friendliest parents but there were days when neither I nor any of their friends would know about their whereabouts. I would dream about it every single night as if it was some sort of hint. My mother would often look as if she was in a daze or was unsure about things but my father was always around assuring her about certain things that we had no clue of.

Ma and Papa were scientists for a multi-national cosmetics company brand known as Aspire. Ma usually used to work from home whereas dad kept on travelling frequently to Japan. We were strictly prohibited from entering their office room and we never bothered to question.

I woke up with a jolt after the same dream kept haunting me, it was fairly early in the morning and everyone in the house was tired so all were sleeping. I decided it was the right time to have a look at mum's office and segregate all the important documents.

"*Rhea beta*"

"*Yes Papa*"

"Sit down"

"What's wrong dad??"

"There are a few things in life that are meant to be known of only at the right time"

"Is everything ok??"

"Yes it is, but if ever anything goes wrong, if someday you feel that now nothing can be worse go to your ma's office and lookout for a little cupboard on the left hand corner of the room"

"Dad are you sure? Won't Ma get angry??"

"As I said when you know that now nothing can be worse than the scenario in front of you, go there, this is the key to that little cupboard" he says and hands me a very small needle like key

"Dad what exactly do u mean buy the worst scenario, for me and Sia you and ma mean everything and when we may lose you'll that might be the worst day which am sure isn't happening soon, so take this key back"

Handing me the key he says "You are wrong, when we die you both will still have a house and funds as well as a lot more people to rely on, then you just have to take away the documents from the upper shelf in the office, only when you realize people around you aren't trustworthy anymore and you aren't safe use this key"

"But Dad tell me what exactly is wrong??" I start dreading his reply, he was always the fun loving and spoiling parent, never once had ye yelled at me or Sia or raised hand and so when he got so serious for the first time in 17 years of my life I knew something was wrong.

"Rhea my child, you are smart enough, you will know what to do am sure just know that I and your Mum will be always around, maybe away for a while but always in your heart"

Nodding my head I hugged him and went to sleep...

Back then I never realized this conversation could have been so important in my life. I headed to the office and unlocked the door with the code, our parents knew that we knew the code still they never bothered changing it and so we never felt like breaking their trust. Using the same code i unlocked the door. A simple mahogany desk stood in the center and nothing looked out of place. Plain white walls adorning mums and Dad's enormous certificates, two huge shelves and that little cupboard in the left hand corner, all of it reminded me of them. Moving towards the table I found a family picture on it. No matter how hard I tried I couldn't believe the fact that they weren't alive anymore and maybe that's the reason I never cried. The picture bought a smile to my face, I quickly moved over to the drawers and opened them, inside were a few documents and a few envelopes too, in the other drawer were also the same kind of stuff along with an envelope saying confidential in bold letters, taking hold of the documents I took another glance around the room and quickly left locking the door while coming out. Immediately I went towards my room I packed those documents in my satchel and moved towards the bathroom to take shower.

"Aunty did Sia wake up?" after shower I headed to the kitchen to find my aunt to let her know about my decision, I had decided to go along with her as we had been familiar with her more than our other family members and I hoped Sia too thought the same.

Sia came soon after and I told her what I had decided, together we told aunt Rakul that we wanted to go along with her and she was more than happy to hear it, I just wished life could be stable for a while.

3 UNWELCOMED

Leaving home I and Sia bid our goodbye's to everyone including the neighboring aunt. Whenever mum and dad used to be out for work Sheila Aunty used to make sure that we ate some home cooked food only, sometimes she even insisted on waiting until mum and dad came back out of generosity but we would somehow convince her that we can manage. Having no children of her own she was highly attached to us especially Sia and made her promise that she would call her every other day.

A stranger was so upset about our departure whereas my grandparents seemed relieved. We were definitely not a burden that's what I thought until Sia playfully said'

"Dadi (paternal grandmother in Hindi) I will come to your house in summer vacations"

"Concentrate on your studies Sia, stop thinking about playing all the time," was grandma's stern reply.

I couldn't handle her unnecessary rudeness and said "Dadi you don't need to worry about her studies, she is still a child, and if you don't want us visiting we won't"

The paternal side of our family never really was fond of us, reason being Grandma's dislike towards mum although there was no particular reason, she just hated the fact that dad married against her will. Thus we never really had those doting grandparents who would spoil us, in fact they would pass on harsh comments when given a chance and so I knew that we would never stay with them no matter what.

Keeping my thoughts aside I headed on to lock the doors. While shuffling the keys I felt as though someone was watching me, I knew it wasn't anyone I knew as everyone was in the backyard. I tried looking around but could only see slight movements in the other neighbor's courtyard; the house had been empty for four years so I dismissed the idea thinking it could be a stray animal.

We reached Gujarat in evening and were glad to be spending time with our cousins; Rakul Aunt was the only person whom we could think of as a guardian and her family as ours. Soon it was decided that I would be joining High school along with my eldest cousin Om and Sia would be accompanied by Tara.

It was always easier for Sia to make friends whereas I topped the introvert of the year list but having Om around made things easier. He was merely two months elder to me and so we were in the same year so I ended up being a new addition to his group although the girls acted weird in the beginning but soon enough I had a set of few friends whom I dearly trusted and still do, similarly Tara helped Sia with the study pattern and she too easily was able to dwell in her surroundings.

Every night I would dream a certain time spent with be a too good to be mum and dad and waking up finding it all true dream I would start sobbing slowly, call it a boon or a bane but I couldn't cry in front of someone which I discovered in the brief period of losing my parents and realizing the fact that they are never coming back. I sometimes wish I could cry in front of someone so they would make me calm down, say all those good things which aren't the truth and try comforting me with their made up facts. For once I wanted to be a kid, someone who could be carefree and not worry about the future.

Still I was happy and content for being in Gujarat, with Om, Tara and Rakul Aunt. Uncle worked for the government that's all we knew and so he was rarely ever home but he would always call and talk to everyone including me and Sia. The call would hardly last minutes but it made us happy thinking at least someone called us. Grandma had just called us once to know that no one would be at their place during the summers so we shouldn't visit; I let her know that we were least interested anyways. I never told Sia about that call and since that day Grandma never called which was a very good thing as i hated talking to her anymore.

She made me realize no matter the blood we shared or the kind of respect my parents had for them I and Sia would be always unwelcomed in their house.

4 HELLO??

"Hello?"

"Hellllloooo??"

After a year coming back to my house I couldn't control the welled up emotion on seeing our house, those rooms where mum would run behind me and Sia playing games and papa would catch us out of nowhere. All those memories seemed real for a moment. I wish they could come back. I cried myself to sleep that day hoping to meet them in my dreams at least.

It's been a month now since I am back here, things have been fairly normal and Sia will be coming here tomorrow as finally her school has ended. Paying bills, maintaing the list of groceries etc has been keeping me busy along with my application to different colleges and a part time job at a book store. Today being Sunday I was trying to get some sleep but maybe that's not what others want. Since morning there has been a few calls on the landline, more like missed calls. Whenever I go towards the living room to answer the call it stops ringing. This being the fifth call I reached dot on time and answered it but it had already ended when I answered it. While going back to sleep it again ringed, thinking of it as some sort of prank I simply removed the chords of the phone and kept it aside.

"Ding Dong"

"Ding Dong"

"First the phone calls and now the doorbell, why don't people let me have a day to myself" thinking of how this Sunday had turned out to be so irritating I reached the door and opened it.

"Pari, sweety what do you want?" she is a cute little kid who happens to be my neighbors daughter.

"Didi (sister in hindi) that bhaiya (brother) asked me to give this to you" she handed me a brown envelope and ran away before I could ask her whom was she talking about.

Closing the door I headed inside and opened the envelope, out fell a few photographs and a letter, all the pictures had two hooded couple walking on a distance, their faces barely visible. I proceeded towards the letter,

"Dear Rhea,

How are you? Of course you are well enough since you are reading this letter. Well first things first the two people you saw in those pictures are your parents."

I sat down and started going through those pictures, I could barely see the faces but I knew it was them, my parents were alive, sobbing I started reading the letter.

"Am sure you might be very happy now but I have a simple question if your parents are alive why haven't they tried contacting you or your sister, maybe because they never wanted you'll or maybe you'll aren't theirs."

The letter ended. Why my parent would's runaway from me and Sia?? And what did it mean by us not being theirs?? Does it mean that I and Sia am not their child or is it some kind of a joke?

It was true that my parent's bodies were never found. The police had searched every possible place but no bodies only blood and that is how they were declared dead but why would they runaway .Is it possible that they don't want us anymore but if so why didn't they contact Rakul Aunt or maybe she just never told us. All this thinking started giving me a headache, popping a pain killer I fell asleep.

5 REALISATION

"Mum why aren't there any baby pictures of me or Sia?"

"Beta (child) your mum was never fond of photography and the few pictures that we might have clicked were lost in fire" dad was the one to reply...

He was the one to reply whenever I or Sia would ask mum a question about our childhood. If ever dad wasn't around and Sia or I would ask whether who was more notorious out of the two of us or who was cuter, mum would simply say, "you both are and will be the most beautiful kids to me."

That's all she would ever say and the topic would change.

Recalling back those moments now I realize that there were a lot of missing elements, a lot of unanswered questions started flooding my mind and so I decided to do some research on my own. First things first,

"Hello Masi"

"Hi beta, how are you, you haven't been calling lately?"

"Sorry, I am good, just have been a bit busy with the college applications and the job at the library"

"Beta you know right that you don't need to work at the library or any other place"

"I know Masi, I am doing it only for experience that's all," truth was I hated being alone at this place, with so many memories of mum and dad I would start crying and feeling helpless so on the insistence and advice of few of my friends I took up this job.

"Ok beta but don't let it affect your studies and take a toll over your health"

"Yes don't worry, by the way Masi the main reason I called you was to tell you that don't send Sia back until I ask you to"

"Is there any problem beta? Whatever it is if you feel unsafe please come back" she said with concerned filled voice but I couldn't tell her or ask her about anything yet.

"No masi no problems, am just busy with the applications and all so till then let her be there as I don't want her to be alone in this house"

"Ok beta as you say, I don't mind keeping you'll with me forever. I will let her know"

"Thank you, I am a bit busy now I will call you back in sometime, bye take care"

"Bye beta, take care of yourself and please if you ever feel unsafe come back"

Unsafe. A very small yet scary word, the question being was I feeling unsafe?

I got dressed to go for my shift in library; it started at 11 am and ended at 5pm, perfectly suitable for me. The Library was owned by an old couple who had a son who lived abroad with his family. They paid me more than needed and I was more than grateful for this job. I had decided that after my shift I will be heading to the police station to ask about any progress in the case of my parents.

I locked the doors of my house properly and started heading towards the library, seeing a fire truck pass by I started thinking about the fire my father used to talk about that broke in our old house. Was there really any such incidence or that too was made up by dad, the only way to find out was by revisiting the old house. I was sure the keys would be in my Mum's office; also I hadn't gotten any calls on my landline in the past hour. Things kept my thinking so occupied that I didn't even realize that I had reached the library and was standing right outside the door. I entered inside only to find a boy around my age sitting on my table with his legs propped upon my desk.

I repeat MY DESK AND MY SEAT that too with those legs of his right beside the pictures of my parents and Sia. He will regret his actions for sure, I walked up to him and looking up close he wasn't as filthy or ugly as I thought with those muscles and all he seemed really good looking. Hiding my expressive thoughts I approached him.

"Excuse me"

"Yes" he said and looking towards me I found him checking me out for a second.

"Excuse me" snapping my fingers in front of his face this time "This is my table you are sitting in"

"And this is my grandparents library you are working in" he had a smug look on his face which only further irritated me. Another addition to the list of jerks in my life.

6 MR. GOLDEN WORDS

Why didn't they tell me that they had a good looking, arrogant but good looking, attitude and all but with charming looks and who keeps on checking me out kind of grandson who was supposed to be coming back today and did I tell you that he is good looking but highly irritating.

God what's wrong with me, I shouldn't be so attracted. *'Rhea don't forget charming boys are bad boys'* I kept chanting that but was broken out of my trance when he started laughing.

"What's wrong with you?"

"What did you just say?" he was still laughing like a maniac

"I didn't say anything, get up"

"Only if you tell me why you think that charming boys are bad boys?" so I said it out loud and had a wide open mouth and he was in a new fit of laughter, I declare it that

I HATE HIM

"Get up or else you won't have a charming face anymore" so what if he is attractive or good looking or has a good physique, I want to get my work done and for that he needs to get up anyhow,

"Use the golden words" he again had that smug look.

"What?"

"The golden words, please and sorry" and now he is trying to be smart.

"If you please don't get up, I will be sorry for breaking your nose" and so I pulled his chair and off he fell, no one acts smart with me and I mean it.

"How do you feel Mr. GOLDEN WORDS?" so he is in pain, it seems he had hurted his foot somehow, I helped him get up and sit on a nearby sofa.

He kept on giving me that look which clearly said I will see you later but it seemed he was moreover enjoying my hospitality. Whenever I would hold his hand or shoulder he would start wailing for no reason attracting the attention of everyone in the library.

"Look, just stop acting as if you are hurt when I know you aren't because this time I will make sure you have a twisted wrist to match with your twisted foot if you don't stop wailing" and that made him shut up.

"Why do you have to be so violent?" trying to act all innocent, he should try acting, Bollywood is his calling.

"Try being an actor, the perfect profession"

"I know I am very good looking and charming but nope I am happier being a lawyer" he doesn't look the beauty with brains type but who am I to judge. Spraying some pain relief spray on his foot which was the only thing in the first aid box I told him to relax.

I got busy saving name of all the needed books and the entire list of home issued ones. I loved this job since I loved books and library was like heaven to me. Sometimes in my idle time I would sit and start reading any book that would gain my interest and would leave it back to its place while leaving only to come back to it the next day. Mr. Golden words had fallen asleep and it was nearly 4 pm now .How will I leave for the police station if he is sleeping that too so peacefully but right at that moment Mr. and Mrs. Katyal arrived.

"So he is asleep, I hope he behaved" Mrs.Katyal had a look of adoration on her face while talking about her grandson, slightly stroking his hair she asked him to wake up

"Yes he was alright" I didn't want to spoil her moment by ranting about the incidences that occurred.

"He is a good child and has comeback to live with us" Mr.Katyal never praised any of his grandchildren's as far as I remember, apart from Gautam. Ohh so he is Gautam I suppose, the favorite kid.

I felt envious because never had my grandparents praised me or Sia but now that I think about it maybe we weren't their grandchildren and so they couldn't treat us as their own. How could I blame them or anyone for that instance?

"Uncle and Aunty now that you both are here and am done with all the work, do you'll mind if I leave a little early" I needed to get to the police station and so it would be better if I left a little early.

"Yes, Gautam will drop you wherever you need to head to" so I guessed it right, Gautam it is.

"No aunty its fine I will be alright" I didn't want him basking me with questions.

"Gautam go with her and don't say no Rhea" and I couldn't so I gave them a nod and left.

Gautam was already walking ahead of me, he just asked me once where I wanted to go to and after hearing my answer kept quiet.

7 CLUELESS

Soon we reached outside the police station.

"Do you want me to accompany you?"

"No its ok, I will be fine"

"Are you sure? Like if you want I can," truth was I didn't want him to know about my parents, I didn't want him to be sympathizing me.

"No I am alright" I was alright, as I knew they were alive. I was curious to know a lot of things and for that I had to be alone.

Giving a nod he left. No goodbyes exchanged.

Reaching inside I headed to meet Officer R.Reddy. He was a short and stout man of few words who always had solved all his cases. My parent's case had wrecked his nerves as the bodies could never be found. He had always been suspicious and I dreaded that he knew something that he never told anyone because he didn't trust any of my family members but now that I was an adult I hoped on knowing it all.

"Good evening Sir" I found him discussing a case with one of his colleagues. I didn't feel like interfering at first but I had waited an entire year and didn't feel like waiting anymore.

"Good evening Rhea, right?" so he does remember me.

"Yes Sir"

"Come sit" he directed his hands towards the cabin.

I sat on the chair beside his desk and waited for him to say something but he never did.

"Sir any leads?" I knew he was a man of few words and so I initiated the conversation.

"Rhea you and I are both aware that your parents were in trouble. It seemed that they were running away from something and so it's a possibility that someone could have destroyed their bodies after the accident so that there would be no clues or evidence left" he was again going through the file of my parent's case. It was a challenging case for him. I trusted him but I couldn't tell him about the pictures or the letter. Not until I am sure about it.

"Sir are you sure about the bodies?" I still doubted the pictures.

"Yes I am. If you come to know about anything please feel free to inform me"

"Yes I surely will and Sir if you ever find out anything please inform me" he had a knowing look on his face he knew that even I didn't trust my family members.

Giving him my regards I left. Reaching on my doorstep I again found Pari with another envelope in her hand and I dreaded opening it.

"Didi, bhaiya gave this for you"

"Thank you Pari"

She was about to leave when, "Pari next time that bhaiya comes ask him to handover the letter to me by himself"

Giving a nod and a cute smile she left. I went inside the house and locked the doors. I sat down to open the envelope only to find a chain, a photograph and another letter.

"I want you to wear this chain, it belongs to you."

The photograph was of a very pretty woman who had the similar chain I was holding around her neck. The woman had the similar kind of features I and Sia did which only made me question myself.

Am I really Rhea Sharma??

8 PRETTY WOMAN

The women in the photograph seemed to be a very prestigious lady, with minimal makeup and a perfectly put up side bun she looked more like an actress of the 80's but with a lot more class and charm to add to her personality. The only jewellery she possessed was that chain and her smile.

The chain was precious which could be easily made out by the ruby dangling to it. It also had certain uniqueness to it. I was inspecting the chain when I found out something engraved over it.

L.V. Hamirani 23kdm A&N

Immediately I opened my laptop and searched for the same name. Pop came a hundred search results out of which the top three were jewellery companies running under the same brand name. On further research I found out that the three companies were owned by three brothers but I intended on finding L.V. Hamirani and so I noted down the number of all the three shops.

I called up to the first branch only to find that luck was indeed in my favor. It turned out that he was present there. I informed them that I was an old customer and wanted a few changes in my jewellery and for the same I would like to talk to Mr. L.V. Hamirani himself. They kept me on hold and later informed that I could visit them right now if possible as the owner would be leaving for Iran tomorrow.

I couldn't take any risks at the moment and so I left the house taking my purse, photograph and chain heading to the first branch. The entire forty five minutes I kept on thinking about how life had taken such a drastic turn in the past one month, about everything that the officer had said about my parents running away from something. Before I could think more about it I had reached my destination.

It was a grand two storey shop with two huge security guards guarding the entrance. I went inside and on asking for the owner I was taken to his office which was on the second floor. A luxurious wooden floored room with glass doors. It had a certain aura to it. I sat down waiting for the man himself when a man asked me if I would like to drink something, I asked for a glass of water. Ten minutes later came an old man on his wheelchair which was being handled by another young man.

"Hello" I stood up and greeted him.

"Hello young lady" he moved forward his wheelchair and asking for my hand placed a kiss upon it. I gave him a smile and he winked back.

It seemed that the old man Mr. L.V. Hamirani was a gentleman and a charmer back in his times.

He told me to join him for coffee to which I politely declined but he insisted that I at least accompany him and so I sat opposite him on his coffee table. Without further adieu I showed him the photograph asking him what he knew about the lady. He seemed shocked for a couple of minutes and kept glancing at me and then at the picture back and forth. He ordered his caretaker to leave his side and close the door upon leaving.

Before I could react the old man slowly got up from his wheelchair and took out another similar looking chain from a locker.

"Yes I can walk and you my lady don't need to tell anyone about it, ok??" I nodded my head in agreement.

"My sons have been constantly fighting with each other for a larger share in property so I had to pretend to be paralyzed to get rid of their constant arguments, I hope you understand," I pitied him as even after being perfectly able to walk he had to pretend being disabled only to maintain peace and harmony among his sons.

"Now the lady and her picture are both something I can never forget because the same picture was used by me years ago to endorse my brand"

"You know her?"

"No I don't, apparently her father wanted this chain made for her and since he didn't want me to create any similar copies of the chain I asked him to give me a picture of his daughter in return wearing the same chain as a token. At first he seemed hesitant but then I told him I want it only as a memory of my work and so he agreed, although later I did create another similar piece which I never sold"

"So you don't have any clue as to who this lady could be, not a single clue?" I had huge hopes while approaching this man but it was all on the verge of shattering.

"I have an address but I am not sure if you will be able to find there anyone. Still I will hand it over to you, you can at least try" the man moved towards the locker and gave me a small folded crumpled paper.

"Thank you so much" I really couldn't thank him enough.

"Thank me when your work is done and when you find your relative"

Relative? I was related to her and so we were related but what was our relation no one knew apart from the one sending me those letters and my runaway parents. I thanked him and was about to leave when he asked me to wait so that he could adjust again on the wheelchair. I started laughing to that.

"You are a young girl, keep smiling and laughing, don't let the hardships in life affect your youth" I walked up to him and hugged him to which he said that I should keep visiting him. I agreed and left with a determined look on my face.

Reaching home I went towards my landline and found 8 missed calls and a message. I decided to freshen up first and then check who is again persistent to get on my nerves. Once I was done with all the little chores I headed to the living room, I pressed the message button and heard.

"Rhea runaway"

9 ROOTS

I woke up drenched in sweat, looking around I realized it was just a dream.

Yesterday after coming back home I didn't realize when I had fallen asleep in my baggy jeans and the same loose t-shirt I had worn to work and later to the police station as well as to meet Mr. L.V. Hamirani. I was so tired that I didn't even turn off the lights but waking up I still couldn't get rid of that dream.

"Rhea runaway"

It was mum's voice. I headed to the kitchen to make myself a quick breakfast as last night I slept empty stomach. Keeping a cup of two minutes noodles in the oven I headed to freshen up. While brushing my teeth I decided to call up Mrs. Katyal and ask her if I could come for an earlier shift so that later I could head to the given address.

I removed the noodles from the oven and moved to the living room to watch TV while eating. When I moved to fetch the remote from the adjacent table I saw my landline continuously beeping but since I hadn't changed the batteries in a longtime there was just the flash of light and no sound. I immediately pressed the button to find 8 missed calls. All weird numbers just like the last time but thankfully no messages. My dream had been partially a reality and so it was getting more necessary for me to find out the truth.

I called up Mrs. Katyal and unlike always she was alright with my arrival timings. Gorging down the now cold noodles I headed to the shower and got under the hot water. It stinged my skin but it brought me back to reality, calming my nerves and making me realize that I needed to dress up decently as I could be meeting very rich people and I didn't want to scare them off by appearing as a little lady druggie in my baggy attire.

I wore a simple one piece that touched my knees, with flowers on it and teaming it up with a pair of flats and a bracelet. I looked like a decent girl. With a touch of kohl and mascara I was ready to head on to the library. I grabbed a bag and carrying some cash, the address, photograph, necklace and those letters. Maybe I could find someone whom I could rely on and tell the entire truth so I wanted to be prepared. Carrying a can of pepper spray I finally found me ready.

I left the house and reached the library in merely 10 minutes. Maria greeted me at the door; she worked from morning 6-11 after which began my shift. She was happy to be leaving early today as she had an important lecture in college which she wasn't planning to miss.

Maria was an orphan who worked part-time at Mrs. Katyal's library for her pocket money, a year younger to me she always seemed cheerful and happy. I kept smiling and walking towards my table only to find none other than Mr. Golden Words again propped on my desk, before I could say something he was quick enough in getting up from my desk and moving towards Mrs. Katyal's desk.

"I was given some work by Maria and so had to use your computer as only yours supported the needed software" he seemed different today, more of an introvert.

"It's alright; you can use my computer and desk for work, I repeat work only" I sat on my desk and started checking the accounts which were updated by him I suppose.

"Why did you update the accounts? You didn't have to do it" it was my work to keep a tab on the accounts; he didn't need to all that work.

"I have been sitting idle since morning, so asked Maria if I could do anything and here it is" Maria will be getting a left and right from me tomorrow.

"Look this isn't your work; you can handle something else alright?" I didn't want to get my work done by someone else.

"I was free, had nothing else to do that is the only reason I did your work" he sounded a little upset.

"Thank you for doing it, but aren't you supposed to be studying?" I knew he was pursuing law and as far as I was aware, lawyers barely had free time.

"I have partially completed my degree in the U.S. Will be starting my course in specialization soon" he looks too young to have completed a degree.

"Aren't you too young to have completed a degree?"

"I am just 21" he winked and I blushed "but since I was a straight A+ student I jumped a few classes and completed earlier than others" he definitely wasn't bragging which could be made out from his confidence level but he didn't seem someone to be with brains. Don't judge a book by its cover.

"That's really good, although you can help in arranging books and making lists to use your idle time"

"Or I could hangout with you if you don't mind" hangout with him, not a very good idea but it can't be that bad either.

Here I have a guy asking me out indirectly when I have so much to unravel on my own. God is great.

Seeing that I was taking time to reply he said "It's ok if you don't want to. It's just that I don't know anyone here and thought maybe you could be my first friend" with a hurt look on his face which I knew was fake he kept ranting about how lonely he felt without a pretty girl in his life. All I could do was laugh, soon he joined me in.

"I will hangout with you"

"I know you will" smug look again.

"But not today" he again made that puppy face and I started laughing.

"You look pretty when you laugh, it's kind of contagious" I smiled and thanked him getting back to work. We would chit chat in between and soon it was time for me to leave.

Mr. & Mrs. Katyal arrived and again they insisted that Gautam drops me to wherever I want to head to, I didn't deny their offer because I needed a little support and for the time being he seemed to be the perfect candidate.

We got ourselves some takeaway food as according to Google map it was an hour long journey. Playing 20 questions and knowing about each other we reached the place. At first I thought it could be a wrong address but upon further confirmation from locals we found that we were at the perfect place. It wasn't a house, it was a manor. In huge words was the name **Rajput Bhavan** engraved on the outer walls of the house.

10 RAJPUT BHAVAN

This definitely wasn't an ordinary person's house and so I was impressed with my decision of wearing decent clothes for the day. I usually wore decent clothes but these seemed more presentable. I turned around to find Gautam and ask him to leave but he was already heading towards the house.

"Excuse me, where are you going?" I turned him so that he was facing me with an awkward expression unlike always.

"Duhh, are you blind or something? Isn't it visible to you that we are heading to the house?"

"I and not we. You are going back." I can't make him a part of my tricky life. The lesser the people involved the easier it would be for me to tackle the situation.

"I am coming and that's final"

"No you aren't. This is my relative's place and I am here to discuss some personal matters so you can't come" he seemed disappointed but I couldn't let him know things, at least not until I was sure about a few things myself.

"Ok then, see ya tomorrow?" more of a question, I know he would be determined to hangout with me.

"Ya I will see you in the library and later we can hangout as well." that seemed to instantly lighten up his sour mood and I didn't knew why exactly but seeing him happy I felt calm.

Maybe because I always felt that I couldn't keep people happy and seeing him happy changed the fact.

"Ok, I will be waiting" winking with his dimpled smile he left.

I was left alone in front of those big iron gates. I didn't know what waited inside but I knew I would be meeting people who might be connected to me and they surely wouldn't harm their own blood now, or will they?

"Madam Aap ko kisse milna hai?" (Madam whom do you want to meet?) The watchman who was guarding the gate asked me with a stern look on his face. I myself wasn't aware about whom do I want to meet but I couldn't give him that answer or he would kick me out before I could even get to know my answers. I looked around and knew instantly how to head inside.

"Bhaiya mujhe Rajput ji se milna hai" (Brother I want to meet Mr. Rajput) he gave me a smile, his stern look fading away and turned around to call over the intercom. The brother trick always works if you know whom to be using it on. The board stating Rajput Bhavan seemed to be an added advantage at the moment.

"Madam Aapko kisne bheja hai?"(Madam who has sent you?) He was still on call and I knew what to be doing now. I immediately took out the photograph and showed it to him. He was shocked and kept looking onto the picture and then at me. He said something to the man on call and ended the conversation with a huge smile on his face.

"Jao beta" (go child) he opened the gates and asked me to go inside. I didn't know what conversation did he have on call but one thing was for sure that the lady in the picture seems to be very helpful for me in getting my answers.

I was greeted on the doorstep by a very old looking lady. Old just in age, she wore a crisp saree adorned with neatly tied bun. She had precious pearls and diamonds around her neck and hands. She kept staring at me and before I could say something or look around she came up close and hugged me. I didn't know how to react as she began crying. I patted her back which seemed to bring her out of her emotional phase.

"I am sorry , it's just that you look so much like Anu that I forgot to even introduce myself" she tried calming herself and got back to normalcy all this was done in elegance and I just kept admiring her for it still thinking about who could be Anu now.

She took me inside and all I could see was beauty. The house was a masterpiece adorned in lots of lights and family portraits. We headed to an upper floor through a grand staircase fit for a palace. The house seemed to be right out of some Yash raj film. On the upper level all I could see were huge corridors which led to a lot of doors. The walls had huge portraits and pictures of the mysterious pretty woman. Few childhood pictures and lots of teenage ones upon closer look you could see the similarity between her and me and Sia which easily justified the old woman's outburst.

"She was a very pretty girl. Every girl used to be envious of her but she never really cared" the lady said walking up to me and looking at the woman's picture with pure adoration.

"Where is she now?" I needed to know where she is.

"We lost her 13 years ago" she had tears in her eyes and yet again I didn't knew how to react so I just hugged her again. She calmed down soon enough and holding my hand took me towards a room at the corner.

The room was fairly lit with a huge bed in centre. I moved towards the bed only to see a frail looking old men lying on bed. The lady sat beside him and held his hand. She asked me to sit on the nearby chair.

"This is my husband Mr. Rajvardhan Rajput and I am Leela Rajput" she said formally introducing herself and her husband whereas Mr. Rajput kept looking towards me and at his wife back and forth.

"We are the parents of Anamika" she added. Upon seeing a confused look on my face she pointed towards the photograph in my hand.

"And this chain belongs to her?" I asked removing the chain from my bag and handing it to her.

"Where did you get this from?" it was Mr. Rajput this time and he looked shocked.

Maybe it was finally time I tell someone the truth.

(Yash raj is a bollywood film making company)

11 ANAMIKA RAJPUT

I told them everything right since mum and dad's accident to the letter but I left out the parts about those documents and the key. They were quiet the entire time only nodding but when they heard about the letter in which I had received the chain and the photograph they seemed to be on top of the world. Mrs. Rajput had tears streaming down her eyes and Mr. Rajput kept on consoling her as well as held my hand.

"Am I in some kind of trouble?"

"My Ramika, still as innocent as always" she hugged me and started blabbering.

"May I know who Ramika is if she is the reason for you guys being so happy?" they stared at me and then started laughing.

"My dear you are Ramika, Ramika Singhania"

"I think you are mistaken as am Rhea and not some girl called Ramika" I forgot to introduce myself, but does it mean they would start addressing me by some other girls name?

"No child, that's not your name. Allow us to explain to you the actual story."

"Anamika was our only child. All this you see was hers. She loved this house so much that every year she would herself form a renovation plan making the house look better than the last time. She was definitely spoiled by us but she never acted like a spoiled kid. No grand demands and no unnecessary arguments.

She was a naturally talented girl. Be it beauty or brains, she always topped the list. A lot of girls would be envious of her but she would only help them in getting better. She was religious and traditional but her thoughts were modern. She only preferred to focus on goals in life and men were in the bottom of her list. She was studying to be a doctor when a male student in her college started stalking her. At first she never really realized but when she did, she didn't know whom to tell about this. She was well aware that if she would tell us we would ask her to comeback or go to college with bodyguards. She hadn't revealed her identity in college and involving us could have done it as well as she didn't want to be favored because she was rich. She preferred being known for her talent and hard-work.

The boy was rich as well, Ram Singhania. His father was the biggest face of cosmetologists in the world and wanted his son to be as famous as him. Ram was a brilliant boy but my daughter had taken of his focus. Soon Ram's father found out about him being interested in Anu and without wasting anytime he approached us. We didn't know how to react so we called up Anu and asked her to come back to Mumbai the next day.

We never knew this until a few years later that Ram had tried attempting suicide in the hostel right in front of our daughter so that she would either be with him or else he would die. Anu started crying seeing Ram holding a blade and when Anu didn't give an immediate answer he cut his hand right in front of her. Not just 1 or 2 but 7 cuts were there on his wrist .Anu immediately called his friends and took him to a hospital where he was treated and took care of. The doctors knew who he was and so they informed his father instead of the police. His father on finding this started begging to Anu that she marries him and she had no other option other than agreeing to a helpless father.

The next day when she was back and we asked her about her decision she simply said yes. Soon they got married. Since she was our only daughter we wanted the wedding to be grand and memorable. Ram being Mr. Singhania's only son he too agreed for the same but had we known that Anu never really was interested we would had never let this marriage happen."

Mr. Rajput sat up and again holding my hand began talking "She was just like water. Pure. She never fought and after getting married to Ram as well she tried her best to prove herself as a good wife."

"Ram was a possessive husband. He didn't like Anu talking to other men and so he would often keep her away from limelight. She wasn't allowed to visit us as well. Only once did she visit us for a month when you were to be born." I knew we were related but

"She was my mother?" I asked with tear filled eyes.

"Yes and she loved you and Sanika a lot" I knew she did as their eyes said it all.

"The day you were born Anu was on top of the world. Soon your father came to visit and he as well seemed happy to have another pretty angel in his life. It was your nani" he said looking towards Mrs. Rajput" who named you Ramika. Perfect mixture of Ram and Anamika. Soon again your mother stopped visiting us. She would always say that it was you who kept her busy and so we would visit her so that we could spend time with you." Mr. Rajput started coughing.

"Mr. Rajput I think you should rest. We can continue some other day."

"Dear we are your nana (maternal grandfather) and nani (maternal grandmother) so don't be so formal" they had a look of longing on their faces. I hugged them both and started crying. This was kind of a reunion although I don't even remember them or their faces but I knew I was in safe hands.

"Madam the food is ready" the maid said entering the room and addressing Mrs. Rajput, I mean Nani.

"Bring it to this room, we will have the dinner with our granddaughter today." the maid left nodding and smiling.

"I will have dinner at home, please don't worry about me. I have work tomorrow and so I should be home and getting some rest" I said getting up from my place.

"Nonsense, you aren't going anywhere. You will be having dinner with us and then will sleep here, tomorrow after listening the entire story you can leave to get you clothes" she wasn't forcing, it was an order and I couldn't deny after seeing them so happy.

"OK I will stay" they seemed to relax at that and I knew my decision of staying back will be helpful.

A lot had been revealed and a lot more was to come.

12 3RD LETTER

"Twinkle Twinkle little star"

"I have told you a lot of times, not to sing with that voice of yours. Are you doing it to attract the boy next door??"

"I am married to you, we have a daughter and still you doubt me?"

"You worthless, pathetic, good for nothing women, don't back answer Me." he slapped her and pulling her hairs took her to the bathroom and locked her inside.

She kept crying and yelling to be brought out. I stood out near the bathroom door crying as well.

"Rami, beta wake up. Rami wake up beta, stop crying please am right here beside you."

I woke up and on instinct touched my face and felt tears. It was a hazy dream but felt too real. I could hear my mother, my real mother begging to be unlocked. In 14 years I never had a dream but it all seemed to be like a lost memory. Nani was still beside me and I was still shedding tears for a very old memory.

It was a conversation between my real mom and dad and if my father is anything like the man in my dreams then I don't ever want to meet that man. Nani was trying her best to keep me calm and it was working already.

"Nani what's the time?" I asked her with my head still on her lap.

"Meri pari sirf 9 baje hain" (My angel it's just 9am) I immediately woke up with a jerk that sprained my neck.

It was painful, very painful.

Currently I am on my way to my house, the house where I feel homely and cozy. It so happened that after spraining my neck I was shouted upon by my grandmother for being so hyper about little things in life and after a 10 minutes lecture I was given an ice pack and told to relax , only then would I get to hear the entire story but then I explained to her that I have a job and I can't leave it without making them aware about it .At first she seemed hesitant, who wouldn't as she had seen me after 14 years and she was scared of loosing me as well after my mother so I explained her that Mr.& Mrs. Katyal were also old and they relied on me for a lot of library work. She seemed to relate to their age and all and so I am here on my way. I definitely couldn't go to work in my yesterday's outfit.

I had exactly an hour left for work, enough time to get ready and get a quick breakfast. Nani will be very angry seeing my breakfast left on the bedside table as it is. I didn't even have a toothbrush and I didn't feel like relying on my fingers at all, so I left it all.

"Excuse me, can't you see and walk?" someone happened to push me and walk away. He seemed to be hurrying of to somewhere but does that mean he will keep pushing people.

"I am sorry" he just said sorry and continued walking away.

I am in a very good mood and I can't let a guy's push affect my mood. I was about to move on when something like a visiting card caught my eye. I bent down and picked up the black colored visiting card. In bold letters was the name written,

Lav Singhania

There was no other information apart from the name and a contact number. The guy was long gone so there was no use in running after him like a maniac. I proceeded upstairs to my flat where I found another letter on the doorstep. This time the person hadn't used Pari or anyone else. I took the letter and headed inside.

My dearest Ramika,

I am sure you have discovered the truth by now. I want to meet you and I will very soon but till then look how I have treated your kidnappers.

There were photographs of my parents, the ones who looked after me and Sia when no one else did. They both had swollen eyes, marks of being hit on face and other body parts, busted lips. They looked scared. I couldn't stop myself from crying. They were in such a bad condition. They didn't deserve any of it.

Is it possible that they might have kidnapped me and Sia? But why would they do that. As far as I remember kidnappers don't treat their captives as princesses and that too for years.

I didn't know what the reality was anymore. Two set of parents and two set of grandparents. All seemed to be so different from one another. My parents are dead but after a year I find that they are alive but running away from someone. My real mother is dead. My maternal grandparents love me a lot. My father who is supposed to be taking care of me keeps sending me horrifying letters.

I headed to the land-line to find a few more missed calls. I don't know why people don't call on my cell phone instead. I hadn't talked to Sia in days; she hadn't called me even once. Immediately I decided that I must go to Gujarat. If those people were my kidnappers and now that they are caught, her life could be in danger. For now I could only rely on one person.

'Hello Gautam"

"I knew you would call" he needs a reality check.

"I need your help"

"Are you alright? He seemed genuinely concerned.

"Do you mind coming with me to Gujarat?' I know I just recently met him. But for now he seemed to be the only real person with a real identity in my life, who wasn't pretending to be someone else and was a lawyer. What more could I ask for.

"When?" He didn't ask me why or for what. No questions were asked and at that moment I knew asking him was the right choice.

"Book the tickets for the earliest flight; we need to leave as soon as possible"

"Ok, I will call you when everything is done" no bye nothing, maybe he understood the severity of the situation and didn't want to waste another few minutes in bidding goodbye's.

Rakul aunt I know you will never harm Sia. I need answers and I am sure you do have a lot to talk about.

13 BURNT DOWN

Departure time is 6pm, meet me at the airport.

Within a few minutes I received this message from Gautam. I started packing all my stuff and decided to leave after meeting my grandparents. I still had a lot of time and I needed to know their side of story. Their house happened to be near the airport which would save a lot of time.

After having packed all the relevant items I left the house. Outside I was greeted by Pari who was busy playing some game on her mother's phone.

"Didi (sister) where are you going?"

"I am going to visit Sia Didi"

"So how will you meet that Bhaiya who brings your letters?" she happens to be a very nosy yet smart kid. She was right, what if I get another important letter. I couldn't drop my plans but I had to keep a tab.

"Didi don't stress yourself, if bhaiya comes I will take the letter for you and call you and inform about it." Smart kid as I said before.

"Pari I will give you a chocolate when I come back but take the letter only in the presence of someone" that man could be dangerous and I don't want anyone to be affected because of me, especially not an innocent little girl.

"Don't worry didi, I watch all crime shows and know that we should only talk to strangers in presence of others."

I shook her hands as in to make a deal. She gave me a salute like a soldier and waving goodbye headed to play with other kids.

Thinking about her antics and carrying my entire luggage I headed to catch a cab for the Rajput Bhavan. The ride unlike always was spent in my dozing off and waking up after the jerk on every speed breaker. After the third jerk I could see myself nearing my present destination and decided to stay awake and alert for the time being.

"You are just like your mother" that seemed to lighten up my mood. I was being greeted by my nani right on the doorstep.

" You didn't bother to tell me you were leaving and didn't even eat your breakfast" so I was in a hurry and knew she wouldn't let me leave without having breakfast so I planned on informing Shyamu Kaka the watchman and leaving instead.

"Am sorry, I really am but for now I want you to complete the entire story"

"Is everything alright? Has something been bothering you?" she took me inside holding my hands to nanaji's bedroom.

"Everything is fine nani, nothing is wrong. I am going to Gujarat for a few days and so I didn't want to leave without informing you as well as knowing the truth."

"Your nani has been blabbering since morning, she was scared that we would be losing you again" Nanaji was trying to act all cool but I could see that even he seemed relieved after seeing me.

"Sorry for troubling you both, but now can we please continue."

"Yes" both nodded and this time it was nani who began.

"Your father had become a doctor by the time you were born and he was gaining name in his field. He was very good at his work. Your mother too wanted to complete her degree but that man never agreed. He was way too possessive and that was the only thing that was ruining their relation. Soon your mother got pregnant again but the child was lost due to some reason which we don't know."

"The lost of your second sibling had transformed your father completely. Anu was immensely shattered but Ram had worse effects. Things weren't very good between your parents until Anu became pregnant for the third time. This time the child was like a key to their new found love. Your father would take your mother out for movies leaving you with us. He took breaks from his work only to look after Anu's health and during the ninth month he sent her here so we could take care of her. Finally he had started opening up to us. We were assured that the new child would be very special and soon was a little angel born. This time it was your mother who named her Sanika"

"So Sia's real name is Sanika?"

"Yes my dear" too many changes were made in my life. But why?

"Your father again started behaving awkwardly for a few days but then soon he was normal. It was all good until the day your house was set aflame," tears started trickling down her cheeks.

I immediately recalled mum and dad talking about our old house being burnt down and now this.

"Your mother was in the kitchen and couldn't be saved" she had a dreamy look on her face and tears kept coming. She had lost her only child and recalling the memory could be very affecting but I needed to know everything and for that she had to speak up.

"You and Sanika were never found. Later it was discovered that your neighbors' had burnt down your house and kidnapped you both .They were disguised so you both couldn't be found. Since then Ram has never been in contact with us. We could understand his grief. He left to live in Japan forever. We haven't yet informed him as we don't know his whereabouts but am sure when he finds out that you both are alive he will be very happy."

"Nani I never told you about Sanika being alive then how did you come to know?" I remember not even once had I taken Sia's name.

"Rakul told me. A year ago after your kidnappers died in a car crash she called us up and informed us that you both are alive. She said that someone was after you two and not your kidnappers so in order to keep you both safe we should let you both be with her. That's the reason when you arrived on our doorstep we didn't ask any questions. We knew Rakul could be trusted as her husband happens to be a trusted government employee and we wouldn't be able to keep your identities intact so we let her take care of you."

"Why didn't you ever talk to us?" I couldn't trust anyone, now not even Rakul Aunt. She is my fake mother's sister yet my Nani trusts her, I could feel a headache coming.

"The phones were being tracked so we never dared to contact. We contacted her via letters and she updated us about you two."

"We know it's hard for you." Nanaji hugged me and I couldn't stop myself from hugging back.

I had lunch with them and before I knew it was time to leave. I bid my goodbyes and was on my way to the airport.

14 BACK TO START

"I will be back from the washroom. Take care of the luggage till then."

Nodding his head he again dozed off to sleep. Our flights had been delayed due to weather issues so it was three hours late now. Gautam was busy sleeping and I thought of reading a book. Already two hours had passed and I was also feeling sleepy so I decided to freshen up a bit.

I headed to the washroom when I felt someone was following me. I looked around to find no one apart from a few people loitering around. I came out of the washroom and found something fishy as there wasn't anyone around anymore. When I was about to leave I saw something beside the door, bending down I found an envelope similar to the kind of envelopes I had been receiving. I immediately headed off to where Gautam was sitting. It was announced that our flights was scheduled to leave in a while. I decided to open the envelope in the flight. But what if there was anything illegal in it. So I tore open the envelope to find another letter so I kept in my bag and waking Gautam we headed to get on our flight.

Gautam had sensed that I was tense and so he had been very quiet the entire journey only prying me with suspicious eyes. I didn't know what was in the letter and so I didn't read it in front of him as my reactions could have given in to his suspicions.

We finally arrived at the Gujarat airport with minimal words exchanged between us. We got in a taxi when he spoke up

"I don't know what we are here for but I just want to know one thing."

"Ok" he was here with me; we barely knew each other still he was helping me out so I could at least answer his one question.

"Are you in some kind of trouble?"

"I don't know, I really don't. I am very thankful to you for coming here with me. I just need answer to a few questions that could be life changing for me. I am not sure about being safe or not."

He nodded his head in understanding and didn't question me further. I had told him the truth. I wasn't really sure if I was in some sort of danger or was I finally being rescued. The letter was still n my bag and I wanted to read it as soon as possible. The question was, was I being followed? If yes then why and by whom. My parents who are also my so called kidnappers couldn't be doing all this as they were already captured by my real father. Amid-st all this thinking I reached my Aunt's house.

"Didii," it was Sia who opened the door and hugged me on seeing me after more than a month's time. I felt good seeing my sister back to complete normalcy. After the death of my parents it was Sia who had been affected the most. She had stopped acting like girls her age but she was getting back on track all cause of my younger cousin Tara who was always beside Sia.

After heading inside I was immediately greeted by my cousins and I introduced Gautam to them. He was already a charmer according to the girls and my brother was acting all protective.

"Om where is Rakul Aunty?" she was nowhere to be seen and I found it odd as she was usually the first one to be greeting people.

"Ma is sick; she has fever and has been resting in her bedroom since morning." I asked him to come beside me with hand gestures and murmured in his ear to assist Gautam to the guest room and help him whatever he needs till then I am with Aunty. He was a little hesitant but I knew he would handle it.

"Gautam am going to check on my aunt till then you can freshen up and have dinner"

"Didi don't worry we will be here to help Gautam bhaiya if he needs anything." Tara was quick enough to reply with a smile on her face along-with a giggling Sia beside her. I could see a help me look on Gautam's face and decided to leave him with them. I was sure Om wouldn't let the girls flirt around.

The lights were off and the curtains were closed. A little bulb in the corner of the room was on which helped to identify the objects inside the room. I headed to the switch board and turned on the lights. Masi was lying on bed looking frail and in pain. Upon seeing me she had a mixed set of emotions on her face.

"When did you arrive? Is everything alright?" she was trying to sit up while asking me all these questions but couldn't. I helped her sit up with a few pillows supporting her back.

"Masi I am alright, I just arrived a few minutes ago with a friend of mine." she seemed to relax a little after hearing my reply.

"I know that you are here to question me."

"Yes I am, I know you know something Masi, I know it's the fact that mums and dad have been caught by my real father that is eating you up."

"You and I both are well aware that they never mistreated you or Sia. I don't know why they kidnapped you or why they changed your identities."

"Masi are you sure about it. If yes then how did you come to know about my grandparents?" she looked tired and upset. Who wouldn't? Her sister and brother-in-law were in the custody of the parent of the kids they kidnapped and here she was taking care of them and also being questioned.

"Your mother had sent me an email the day they both died or you could say vanished. The letter stated that I was to inform your grandparents about you both but not let you know about it. I was also asked to give you a certain envelope which I left at your house by mistake while coming back to Gujarat. The only thing I know is that they wanted to save you both from someone and that's the reason they decided to vanish but here they are caught up by your father." she started sobbing. I couldn't ask her not to cry when there was no other option left for her.

"I am sure they haven't done anything and I will do my best to save them." I tried comforting her with my words.

Sia entered with bowl of soup for Aunty and left. I helped aunty in having her soup and gave her medicines afterwards. Soon she fell asleep and I headed downstairs.

After having my dinner with everyone we chatted for a while and then everyone retired for the night. I headed to the room Gautam was given

"Do you need anything?" he was lying on bed and got up seeing me.

"All my needs were taken care of by your dear sisters." he made a horrendous expression and I started laughing hearing the way he said it. As far as I knew my sisters, especially Tara I am sure she would have even insisted that he call her up personally if he needed anything. It was healthy flirting and she thought there was no harm in it.

"Don't worry, we are leaving tomorrow evening so just bare with them until then."

"Is your work done already?" he had a quizzical look on his face.

"What I might be looking for apparently lies in my house according to my aunt so I need to get back soon."

"And what about your aunt, is she alright?"

"She will be soon. I will take you tomorrow to meet her, till then rest." passing smiles to each other and wishing good nights I headed to my room.

I changed into my night-suit and looked out for the letter in my bag.

"Dear Ramika,

Don't lookout for answers when you don't know what exactly you are searching for. Don't waste time. I am coming back for you both.

I don't know what's coming for me but whatever it is I will be prepared for it.

15 KEY

"So Gautam, are you and Rhea dating?" that was one embarrassing question especially when we barely knew each other.

I couldn't sleep well the entire night and only kept thinking about who could be coming for us. The thought kept pestering me that something or someone awaits us when we get back to Mumbai. After waking up in morning I took a warm relaxing shower and headed downstairs for breakfast only to find everyone else including my aunt present there. She seemed to be enjoying Gautam's company, in-fact they all did.

We all were having a good time. For once even I had forgotten about my parents and the mess that awaited us back in Mumbai. It was a good moment and all started clicking pictures in their smart phones that's when aunt popped up the not so good question.

"Aunt, I proposed her but she denied." with a frown upon his face he acted as if he really did propose me. He deserves an Oscar for this performance.

"Rhea he is a good guy, why did you reject?" my aunt was giving me a look that stated you have to be with him, he is perfect. So now I had to act as well.

"Masi he has three girlfriends already, I wasn't interested in being the fourth one." and that did it. Everyone waited for his reply with anticipation, eagerness and anger on their faces. Poor Gautam, plan backfired. Hell yeah!!!

I acted as if I was wiping a few stray tears and he was left speechless.

"How dare you try to mess up with my sister?" Om held Gautam's collar and with fury headed on to hit him. Well I was enjoying the current scenario but realizing that things could get heated up I got in between.

"Let it be Om, he has broken up with those three girls now and is trying to prove that he only loves me. That's the reason he is accompanying me," Om calmed down, masi looked happy, Tara and Sia were no more interested in him and Gautam, well he just looked shocked. Finally he will stop flirting I suppose.

Everyone got back to eating and discussing about the next day when suddenly masi got a call,

"Tara, Om and Sia pack your bags. Gautam I trust you with Rhea. We are heading to Dubai, pack everything. We are leaving soon." without waiting for any reactions she ended the call and headed to her bedroom.

"Masi what's going on?" I followed her to her bedroom before she could shut the bedroom door. She took me in and locked the door.

"Your parents have runaway. Your real father is again searching for them. Since you are getting letters from him it proves he knows your location but he isn't aware about Sia and so your grandparents have suggested that I leave." she was shivering, she didn't seem alright but keeping her eyes on the ground she continued talking and packing her bag.

"But Masi I am here, if they are following me won't he know that Sia is my sister."

"No he won't since Sia is our daughter now according to the documents and so we won't have any issues." she looked up and with a dreamy look said," Please take care of yourself, I don't know for how long we will be gone. All I know is that you must get back to the house as soon as possible. Look out for the letter." she got back to her packing and I as well headed to my bedroom.

We all were done with packing in merely two hours. I and Gautam were ready before everyone as we didn't really have anything to pack. Masi asked us to leave before them so that no one found anything suspicious as according to her I was being followed. I bid my goodbyes to everyone.

"Sia, be good to masi. Don't ever upset her. We all will be together soon enough, till then am sure Tara and Om will take good care of you."

"I miss mum and dad." she hugged me and tears fell from her eyes. I asked her to calm down and go along with everyone. She nodded and went to sit beside Tara. Gautam was gifted a box of chocolates by the girls and in return he hugged each one of them at which they blushed. Om too shook hands with him and said something to him which made Gautam relax a bit. Masi asked me to check my cell phone after I get on plane and we left.

After boarding our flights for which tickets had already been booked by my grandparents I checked my cell phone only to find a message from my aunt.

"Delete *this message after you are done reading. We are going to some place that I can't tell you about as you might be questioned later;*

I lied about the place being Dubai. I won't be calling you until things don't settle down back there. Take care of yourself and don't worry about Sia. Date Gautam as he seems a nice guy. :)"

I immediately deleted the text and continued acting normal. Soon we reached Mumbai and I headed to my house. Gautam insisted on accompanying and I couldn't say no.

I entered my house and locked the door. I asked Gautam to relax whereas I headed to mum's office. I spotted the unusual looking envelope on my mother's desk. I tore it open and started reading it.

"I didn't imagine writing this letter as I thought it won't be needed but now if you are reading it I think I made the right decision. We are in danger, specially you and Sia. We are unfortunately not your real parents. Your mother died trying to save you two. Your father is a mad man and so we had to kidnap you in order to save you two. If ever we go missing we will give you missed calls on the landline number. You are never to call back on the number. If the calls are more than five it means that its time you open the little cupboard. If they are three it indicates that we will be dead soon. I can't explain everything to you but always remember, though we weren't your real parents we will always love you two."

Those missed calls were a hint.

I ran to the living room to again find 6 missed calls on the land-line. Gautam had fallen asleep in the mean time and I was thankful for that. I got back to the office and took out the key from my purse. I opened the little cupboard only to find a little attic. I knew things were about to unravel soon. I had already started dreading the truth.

16 ATTIC

I was a little apprehensive. I had never been allowed to enter mum's office which indicated that whatever we would find inside wouldn't be good for our innocent eyes and today am here about to unravel it all. I was scared and hesitant as well. I wish aunt could have accompanied me but she has to take care of three kids out of which one isn't even related to her.

Keeping all worries aside I went to the living room and decided to wake up Gautam. If he is here to help then he should be doing it. I am sure he won't ask any immediate questions as well as I am not sure what I may find down so it's better if I have company.

"Yes Yes I am awake." I had just shaken his shoulder once and he was already up.

"You need to come with me to the office, I have found something." Immediately he got up and we headed to the office.

"What is this? An attic?" he seemed shocked, who wouldn't. I had an attic in my house and I didn't know about it, well the house I live in isn't actually my house so that kind of makes sense.

"Yes it is an attic and we are heading inside to see what could be there."

"Take two torches, your cell phone and a bottle of water."

"Why do we need all that, we aren't going camping."

"You haven't been up there so you don't really know what awaits you so why not be prepared in case we get locked inside."

"How do you know am going there for the first time?" I didn't even tell him about it.

"Well people don't get scared to go to places in their own house until and unless they never really knew about it or were restricted from heading to the particular part of the house." he is definitely way smart.

"I am a lawyer; I look into every aspect which means I am good at observing things." I nodded and went to get torches and my cell phone whereas he headed to get a bottle of water.

Locking all the doors and windows we headed to the office and inside the attic. I soon found a switchboard which had a number of switches. I turned on the biggest switch and heard a certain noise.

"Do you hear that, it seems as if a lot of locks are opening up one by one?"

In merely 20 seconds the entire room was alight. It wasn't a normal room more like a science laboratory.

"What did your parents exactly do?" Gautam was eyeing the entire room with his eyes wide open and so was I.

"Now that I see all this, I don't really know."

The room had a few small shelves and tables. We both headed to discover things. I went to the table and Gautam went near the shelves. The desk was filled with documents. I was going through them when, "Rhea come here, you really need to see this." I went to him to find him closely examining a few glass jars on the shelves.

"These are specimens of my parents."

"I know but aren't they supposed to be dead and later bodies are to be preserved?"

"Yes" I was about to head to the table when he said, "But they are all alive."

"What?"

"See this squirrel." He pinpointed to a squirrel in a jar. At first I couldn't really make out if it really was a squirrel or wasn't but later I could make out that it actually was alive with its slightly open eyes and everything.

"I don't know why these little beings are kept like this. Get aside from it." We got away from that creepy shelf and I again went to the table. I started going through all the documents when I again found an envelope which had confidential written over it. I tore it open. Too many letters in my. I found a few blood reports which I found out to be mine and Sia's.

"Rhea, why are your blood samples here in this box?"

I went to find him holding a huge Thermopylae box which had a few blood samples, whereas Gautam was holding my blood samples I found another one with the name Lav. I recalled that particular visiting card with the name *Lav Singhania* over it. There could be many more Lav's in this world but I had a nagging feeling that there is something fishy about this place as well as that guy Lav. I also found many more blood samples of different guys and girls. The samples were kept in a certain arrangement. Gautam was still going around and exploring stuff. Bringing him up here was indeed a good idea. I kept the box aside and started looking around.

"Were your parent's scientists?" he was going through a book, more like a folio and I was again having a look at the papers in the envelope.

"I don't really know what they were. I didn't even know who I am until a few days ago." I didn't say the other half out loud but I think he heard it.

"You are weird and so am I but what I found now seems to be weirder than anything else." I went up to him to find a box full of nails. The nails seemed to have been removed from a person's body as I could still see dead cells and traces of blood over them. I still couldn't make out anything out of all this.

The nails were all in packets.

"Do you see, they have been removed from an alive person's body so that they can be replaced and start growing again."

"What do you mean?" he handed me a file. The words were too scientific for my understanding but the images clearly made out the purpose. The images showed the nails and how they could be put up on someone else's hands. I felt gross. How could I be living with such people and why do they have my blood samples and everything. All this was giving me a headache and so I decided to get back with a little more insight to all this but first I need to contact Lav. He is definitely related.

I asked Gautam to leave and he agreed as I could see even he didn't really like being up here. I didn't know what more would I find in up here so I decided to go to Rajput Bhavan as I would be safe there but what if mum and dad decide to contact me. After seeing all those things I don't feel like even meeting them.

We took all our belongings as well as those blood reports and a few other documents and headed downstairs. I tried opening the door but it wouldn't budge.

"Now try it." Gautam turned off the huge switch and the door as well opened up whereas the room was dark once again.

"Thank you." I didn't know what exactly I was thanking him for, opening the door or being here with me.

"You don't have to thank me, just say yes." he gave me a flirtatious smile and winked.

"I forgot that I am thanking the wrong person; I take my thank you back."

"I don't need your thank you baby, am just doing all this to prove my love."

"Do you want me to throw you out of my house?"

"Sure, just don't forget about the things upstairs." and that made me shut up.

"Let's go out to eat something, this place is giving me creeps."

"I agree."

I knew this was just the beginning.

17 BROTHER

"You want me to drop you off somewhere?"

"Yes if you can I would like to go to my Nani's house and you too can come in this time."

After having dinner we were too tired to think about anything else and so we decided to get back to all this mess tomorrow. It was easier to hangout with Gautam as he always had something new to talk about and kept the conversation alive and interesting. I didn't mind introducing him to nana and nani as I knew I had finally found someone whom I could trust as well as rely on. He dropped me off to Rajput Bhavan and left.

I headed to the gate only to find two more guards guarding the main gate. I was asked to get inside immediately and I did that exactly only to find a lot more guards guarding the interiors. I found nani on call and before I could even say something the conversation seemed to have ended.

"Your father will be visiting us very soon. He wants to take you along with him."

"But why. I am not ready to go with him."

"You don't really have a choice. We don't have a choice."

"What do you mean Nani?"

"If you don't go along with him he will tell the cops that it was your grandfather and I who got you kidnapped and he will also find your sister. I don't know what are we supposed to do at this age. We did whatever we could but it still doesn't seem enough." she started crying. It was easy to make out that she felt helpless but even before I could move on to console her I heard the honking of a car. Nani came out of her trance and we both moved on to see who had arrived.

He had an aura of a very respectable man. Crisp and perfectly tailored suit adorned with well polished shoes. It could be made out he was rich, very rich. He was accompanied by a young men and a lot of bodyguards. He came inside and touched my Nani's feet. The same gesture was repeated by that man. He seemed to be around my age with a well built physique. He was also dressed up like my father although he had a darker complexion it went along well with his looks of a mafia.

Suddenly I was hugged by "my real dad" note the sarcasm.

"You look just like your mother." he had tears in his eyes and I could see that he was happy to be reunited with me. Upon looking up close I could see the tired look on his vary face. With graying hairs he still managed to look young enough. He asked the guy to come forward.

"Beta he is Lav. He is your brother." Lav. Lav Singhania and it clicked. He is the same guy whom I got pushed by that day but how is he my BROTHER???

"I found him at an orphanage and decided to adopt him after seeing he was a very smart kid. He is very special to me." I could see that he had a certain attachment towards Lav. I and Lav shook hands and we all sat down on the sofa.

"How are you aunty?"

"I am good enough. How have you been?"

"I have coped up well enough. I am very happy to have found out Ramika. I wish Sanika was also alive but we don't always get what we wish for."

"I understand. You lost your wife in that fire and after years you are re united by one of your daughters."

"Yes am very happy and so I have decided to take Ramika with me to Japan. I don't want to risk her life anymore. As you know that her kidnappers have again runaway I don't want to take any chances this time."

"I need a day or two and then we can leave." I didn't know why I felt the need to stay for a few days but I just didn't feel like going yet. As if there were a few things that still had to be discovered by me. A part of me wanted to go ahead and find out what exactly was he doing and why whereas my mind asked me to stay back and be patient.

"Alright you have two days. On the third day we will be leaving." he got up hugged me and left with Lav.

He left two of his bodyguards outside the door and left with the remaining troop. He wasn't a man of emotions. Cut to the chase was his kind of approach. I don't believe him to be the romantic types as Nani says and I still couldn't really trust anyone. I had just two more days and after that I won't have the choice of deciding my fate anymore. I didn't want to risk Sia's life nor anyone else's and so I decided I can't waste any more time.

I bid Nani and Nanaji goodnight and headed to the bedroom I had fallen asleep in. Right then I found a door at the end of the corridor. At first I didn't feel like going to it but then something just provoked me and I headed to the room.

The room's lights turned on the moment I opened the door. It didn't take me long to figure out that it was my mother's room. I closed the door behind me. It didn't seem like a dead person's room. With mahogany wooden flooring and off white walls the room was more like going back in time. A huge shelf was covered with books whereas on the other corner of the room was a huge walk in closet. The walls had lots of pictures of my mother. There was a picture of my mother holding two babies. I could make out the babies as me and Sia. She looked happy.

There was another picture with a huge house in the background. As far as I remember according to my kidnapper's the fire had burnt down my previous house. I moved on to another picture and it left me astounded. There were a lot of people in the picture. The picture seemed to be taken while on a picnic. The people who first caught my attention were my kidnappers. They all looked happy and it could be made out that they all knew each other.

I went to my room and called up Gautam.

"Don't you realize its night and people could be sleeping?" he answered the call in the fourth ring and I could make out by his voice that he was actually sleeping.

"I am really sorry but I really need your help"

"Don't be sorry. Is something wrong?"

"Will be if I don't do anything soon enough."

"What do you mean?'

"Can you somehow find out Ram Singhania's old residential address?"

"Sure, but why?"

"That's where we are going tomorrow morning."

My grandparents were trying to keep me safe but their dual approach wasn't really working. At one point my father is a very good man but at the other he isn't. I needed answers and if people don't answer me, I am sure places will.

18 OLD ABODE

Ram Singhaniia's old house was way famous then I could have imagined. Also, the fire that broke out in that house was in news for a long time as a culprit was never found. Search engines always come in handy. I just had to type my father's name and there it was. There wasn't too much about him. The fire happened to be the major turnover in his life as he had lost his wife and kids in the fire. There was also something about the neighbor's house being burnt down but there was no description about them and neither were they interviewed or were their names mentioned.

I had being doing my share of research the entire night. I couldn't fall asleep. Two days, that's all I had in my hands and I couldn't waste any time in lazing around. Sleep could come once I had the adequate amount of knowledge about my personal life. The only problem that I could be facing now would be the bodyguards but I knew how to tackle them. At one point of time I was determined on letting them accompany us but I still wasn't sure who was the actual threat here and so I couldn't risk any amount of information being let out from my side.

At 6 am I decided to invite Gautam at house. The plan was to dress up as one of the maids and leave the house. Around 5:30 am I started puking or you could say I enacted to be puking. Everyone in the house got tensed and they decided to call a doctor when I texted Gautam to arrange a fake doctor and he did the needful. By 6 he came along-with one of his friends acting as a doctor. I had to act sick but seeing the fake scenario in front of me I had to keep myself from laughing.

"Doctor what's wrong with her?"

"As you can see she has been stressing herself a lot lately and needs ample amount of rest. I have prescribed a certain herbal medicine which you can get only at the huge Ayurveda clinic which is at the end of the town. Gautam and one of your maids can go and get the medicine."

"Doctor but why ayurvedic medicine. Can't she consume any other medicine?"

"Look aunty she is very young. High intake of medicines from a younger age can lead to failure of organs which am sure is something you don't want." Nani still seemed hesitant and Gautam could see that.

"Nani Rhea has a past history of ayurvedic medicines only. She is more used to them so I suggest you give in to the doctor's advice." the statement ended with his charming yet caring smile and I could see nani easily falling for his words.

"Ok, if you insist son you and Reema may go and get the medicines."

"Aunty I am giving her a dosage of a particular medicine which will control her sickness for the time being as well as she will be in deep sleep for now. Don't wake her up until the medicines have arrived. You'll don't have to worry about her."

"Nani can you please send Reema upstairs so she can help me change into a pair of tracks and then her and Gautam can leave."

"Ok beta, I will be with your grandfather. Nancy will come and check upon you if I can't."

"It's ok nani."

The plan had been planned accordingly. Nancy and Reema were both trusted maids of this house and it took me a lot of time to convince them but both agreed once I bribed them with the promise of showing them latest bollywood movies. I know not a very good thing but I had too. I changed into Reema's clothes and asked her to sleep on my bed. The so called Doctor had parked his car right outside the doorway so we all got inside the car without being looked upon by anyone. The timing proved to be perfect as the bodyguards were busy having breakfast.

"This is Neel Roy" Gautam introduced me to his friend.

"Hi. Needless to say you acted really well."

"He is a real doctor." Gautam gave me a stern look whereas Neel was in fits of laughter.

"You are the granddaughter of the Rajput's. Id cards are checked of visitors. So I couldn't risk getting in a fake doctor."

"Am sorry and thankful as well." I took off the salwar kameez as I was already dressed in decent sleeveless kurti n jeans beneath.

We generally chit chatted until I reached my old house. Neel left us there and headed off to his duties promising to be back in an hour. It was still early but what I could make out was that the area was a posh locality. There were small bungalows only and a few people were jogging here and there.

I went to my abode. It could be made out that something bad had happened here. The house next to it also had the same kind of aura oozing out of it, probably being the neighbor's house according to search engines. I took out a bobby pin and headed to the backside of the house. As I had guessed there was a door there as well. I started using my luck and my pin to open the door.

"You are lucky to have been accompanied by a lawyer."

"And you are lucky that am not in the mood to break your nose."

"Why are you always sooo angry?" he kept looking here and there. I know he was trying to make sure that no one notices us and right at that moment the door got unlocked.

As always Mr. Golden words had brought all the necessary items and so taking our torches we headed inside.

The house was dark only a little amount of sunlight got reflected from one of the windows. We could have easily opened up the curtains but we weren't here to be found out or make our presence obvious. A few rats were running here and there. The walls had burn patches. The furniture's were also partially burnt. We headed upstairs and entered the first room which turned out to be mine and Sia's.

"This house can still be maintained as only the walls have been ruined and the lower portion whereas the upper area seems alright." Gautam had been having a close look at everything. The house actually looked alright apart from the lower portion. Although the upper area had a scary touch to it. The house had been stranded for years and as far as I could see most of the belongings were left untouched. There were a few pictures of me and Sia which I kept inside my sling bag without being noticed.

"What do you think could have actually happened here?"

"I am a lawyer and not a detective."

"I know but the way you examine things it confuses me sometimes."

"Well I wanted to be a detective but it had too many cons so I left the idea."

"Ok. Let's go to the other room."

The other room we headed to was more like a bachelor's pad. As if it was only my dad's room. I recalled the fact that mum and dad used to have arguments and so it could be possible that they had separate rooms. Whereas mine and Sia's room still had belongings, Dad's room on the other hand was completely empty and so we headed to the other room.

"Do you know every house has a story?"

"I wish houses could speak."

"They do, everyone has their own way of expressing and a house too has its own."

We were in mum's room. My intuition had been right. A few things were missing whereas the closet was still full of her saree's. I knew I will be finding something here and I wasn't wrong. I started looking here and there and looking at me Gautam too started looking out for something unusual. I went to the depths of the closet when I found a huge painting.

"Gautam please help me with this"

The painting was of me, mum and Sia.

"Mumma why is there no papa in this painting?"

"Because this painting is a secret for my little princesses"

"Secret?"

"Yes, when mumma goes away you take this painting away with you."

"Mumma no go away."

"Yes my baby."

It had been like a triggered memory again. I took the huge box shaped painting and asked Gautam to leave. We immediately headed downstairs and locked the door. Neel was out there waiting in his car. I kept the painting inside and stepped out of the car.

"Do you mind pretending to be my fiancé?"

"Babe I am your fiancé."

"Let's get to work then."

Memories never truly fade away...

19 NEIGHBORS

"What am I this time?"

"Well you can be the driver"

"Or his brother"

It was decided that I and Gautam will visit few of the neighboring houses as a newly engaged couple who plan on shifting in the Singhania's old abode. Poor Neel had left his hospital duties for us and now Gautam was suggesting that he acts as our driver. I didn't want Neel to feel left out so I suggested on him tagging along as Gautam's elder brother instead which left a frown on Gautam's face but he still managed to look cute. Well I am a normal girl and yes he is good looking and smart and chivalrous and...

"Are you done checking me out?" Gautam had lost his frown and it was replaced with a smirk now.

"Why are you so full of yourself? I was looking at the house back there." beware Rhea next time. You can always check him out but see to it that you don't get caught. Yes that could be done.

"Because all of me loves all of you" he suddenly held my hands and started singing the song and before I could whack him, he directed his eyes towards a house which was closest to the Singhania's wherein a woman had been standing on her window and intently having a look at the three of us.

I encircled my hands around his neck, something that I shouldn't be doing but had too.

"I think we should be visiting that house" I still had my hands around his neck and him and Neel understood that it was time to get to work.

Holding hands we started walking towards the house. It was one of those moderate houses but was lacking maintenance. It was the third house in a row, whereas the first one was that of our old neighbors and second one was ours. Both the houses had been affected by the fire but it could be made out that the impact had been on this house as well.

"Yes?" it was the same lady who had been on the window who opened the door on the third bell. She had partially opened the door through which we could only see her face. She looked pretty but weird at the same time with thick bushy eyebrows but a small nose and perfect lips. She had a few scars on her faces which had faded away but not completely as the sunlight highlighted its severity we could make out that she had been wounded badly in the past.

"Hello, I am Gaurav and this is my fiancé Shweta. We are actually planning to shift next door and thought it would be good to know a few of our neighbors."

"Sorry but I am not interested in knowing any of you'll. Bye." and with that she closed the door bang on our faces.

"Well that was weird." Neel was kind of taken aback by her behavior whereas Gautam seemed unfazed.

"We will head on to a different house." I started moving to the next house when Gautam stopped me and handed me a ring.

“If we are acting as engaged couple there should at least be a ring on your finger.” understanding his point I wore the ring although it barely fitted even on my thumb.

“Why don’t we go to that house instead, it also has a beautiful garden” Neel pointed towards the house that was opposite to ours. The house actually looks pretty from the outside. It looked like an actual house instead of the showpieces that covered the entire locality. It had a cozy feel to it and I knew we should be visiting that house instead. There hung a huge board with the name **Saini’s .**

“Hellooo there” so the house wasn’t just pretty but also was owned by a really handsome looking man who also happened to be checking me out, making me blush profusely. After Neel’s advice we agreed upon it and headed to the cozy house and on ringing the bell was greeted upon by this Greek god.

“Hey there, I am Gaurav and this pretty lady here is my fiancée” he held me by waist and started introducing us. Why did I have to act as his fiancé that too today, bad decision “and he is my brother.”

“Son, who is on the door?” I could hear a woman approaching the door.

“Hello aunty, we are soon to be shifting in that house” I pointed towards the house, “As we are new in town and don’t really know anyone we decided why not start by greeting our neighbors.”

“That was a very good thought, come on in.” with a warm smile she welcomed us into her beautiful house.

“Aunty you have a really beautiful house.” Neel was awestruck by the interiors and so were we. It was designed in a cottage style with complete wooden flooring and huge glass windows. Minimal furniture, white walls and a small waterfall in the corner.

"Thank you sons, Jai please get them seated comfortably. I will be back with your father."

"Shweta, right?"

"Yes" I was delighted that he remembered, although my fake name but at least he did.

"Aren't you too young to be engaged already?" I felt like saying nooo am not engaged, but I couldn't.

"Age is just a number you see." and there he is again, he held me protectively as if I was actually his fiancé, why does he have to answer the questions directed to me. Gautam you are surely getting a whack on your head.

Aunty was back with uncle and they both made a lovely couple. I could see where Jai had gotten his looks from. Oh yes I remember his name, I had been paying attention as well. A few servants bought in lots of trays full of food.

"Aunty you didn't have to do all this" and now he is trying to be a gentleman whereas Neel had already started gorging on chips and samosas which kind of made me laugh.

"You kids looked so famished. I could see that you'll had travelled a lot and specially him" Neel suddenly looked up from his eating business and aunty was like "its okay beta, you eat." Gautam gave him a stern look at which he just shrugged and continued eating.

"So where are you'll from?" uncle was a short but fit man. It could be seen that he still went to the gym but yet he was a very soft spoken man.

"Uncle we are from Bangalore, but since I got a job here in Mumbai I decided to shift here with her. We will shift here after our marriage" he started looking in my eyes and for once I felt as if he was trying to convey something.

"It's hard to find true love these days, I am happy that you two decided on getting married." aunty was gushing upon the idea of me and Gautam getting married which was never going to happen, especially after meeting her son.

"I heard you have decided to shift in the opposite house?"

"Well yes uncle." Gautam's reply wasn't expected by them maybe because they looked a bit taken aback.

"I would suggest you kids to lookout for some other place. This house isn't good for a new beginning."

"What do you mean aunty?"

"When the Singhania's had moved into this place they looked as happy as you too, but time took away all their happiness. I don't blame the house but I don't want you two to be suffering the same kind of fate anyhow." Aunty had gotten emotional and had a fazed look on her face.

"We visited their neighbor and she banged the door upon our faces, also a lot of people told us not to shift in there but no appropriate reason. We would like to know what is the reason why no one wants us shifting there." the atmosphere seemed tense everyone was quiet waiting for aunt or uncle to speak. Jai too looked keenly interested and Neel had finally stopped eating.

"The lady you visited happened to be Mrs. Singhania's best friend. According to people she finds herself guilty for her death and that is why she solicited herself after she died."

"Mrs.Singhania was the perfect example of beauty with brains. We were all part of the same social circle. Anamika was a woman everyone wanted to be friends with whereas Ram was so arrogant that once in a party we made fun about him getting someone as a wife whom he never deserved. It was a joke to which Anamika giggled. In a while they left. When we came home at midnight while parking our car we heard a blood curdling scream from their house I insisted on checking upon them but your uncle denied. For a month we never saw Anamika and when we did she had a plastered leg. It was later that we came to know that he had broken her leg cause according to him she was publicly making fun of her husband." Aunty had tears in her eyes "I wish I had intruded on the right time."

Jai bought a glass of water for aunty and Uncle started patting her shoulders.

A samosa is a triangular wheat flour pocket filled with spicy potato or chicken filling which is later sealed and fried, commonly available in Asian countries especially in India and Pakistan as snacks.

20 NEIGHBORS 2

"Your aunty and Anamika were also good friends that is the reason she gets affected every time she happens to think about her," Uncle was the one who decided to tell us about my parents. Upon our insistence aunty had headed to her room to rest and so he continued from where aunty had stopped.

"We are all part of the rich and famous but amongst all of us Ram was on the top. He was lucky as he had such an idealistic person as his father and a woman who the world would envy kind of wife. The woman you visited is Suman Srivastava. Suman was a lawyer and also used to work for NGO's. Suman, my wife and Anamika soon became friends as I, Ram and Anuj, Suman's husband happened to be childhood friends. Ram was always the aloof kid since back then. We don't know how they met and suddenly when did they decide to get married but it was easy to see that Anamika wasn't happy with the entire arrangement. I didn't understand, couldn't her parents make out that she wasn't willing for it?" it seemed as if uncle was questioning himself rather than us. He was blabbering a lot of things but moreover to himself.

"Uncle are you alright?"

"Beta I or none of us know what exactly happened in that house. When the house was set on fire it was around 3-4 am and we all ran towards it. Using the taps and pipes in our garden we controlled the fire easily and we still couldn't understand how she died. She was burnt, from head to toe." Uncle had tears in his eyes, "as if she had been burnt alive. We never heard her screams but what we saw wasn't a pleasant sight. Suman and my love fainted on site and we men couldn't even cry. We called the police only to realize that Ram was in Japan by the time and the kids were never found. Nor were Aniket and Parul." we all had tears in our eyes. I was in a stance but came out of it after recalling the names of my fake parents.

"Uncle Aniket and Parul?"

"Beta they lived in the first house which also remains isolated till date. We don't know where they went. They had shifted a few weeks before the fire and before we could know them they were gone."

"Thank you uncle, we will be leaving now and won't shift in that house that's for sure. Take care of aunty."

"Beta don't tell anyone what we told you." bidding good byes and saying take cares we left.

"Why do you keep visiting weird places?" we were now going back home when Gautam for the first time questioned me.

"Well weird I love weird places." and that ended the conversation. I just wanted to go home and carefully have a look at that painting which currently lied in the backseat. I again wore the clothes and soon after reaching home went straight to my bedroom. I was back on bed and Nani soon entered the room.

"Is she better now?"

"Yes nani am feeling better now." she relaxed at that and soon they all left apart from Gautam.

"Shouldn't you be leaving?"

"Don't you think I deserve to know what I have been doing illegal works for?"

"I have a very complicated life, for now what I can only tell you is I am Mr. Singhania's daughter."

"Let me know what our next step is." and with that he left. I was none other than the famous Ram Singhania's daughter and granddaughter of the Rajput's yet my life was in danger. I was born with a silver spoon but living the life of the clay spoon ones.

After having my lunch I convinced nani to take a nap. I headed on to the painting and started thinking why don't I remember things about my mother. Why do I get flashbacks?

The painting was created by my mother but it had a very odd structure as well as it was a little heavy. The paint was still glowing and that's when I noticed a little uneven spot on our noses. It was on the noses of all three of us. I touched the noses one by one only to here a click at the end when I touched my nose. I turned around the painting and found a compartment in the frame which had unlocked. I opened it to get a box. Upon opening the box I found a diary within. A rugged looking diary. I kept the painting back to its place and closed the compartment and headed with the diary towards the bed as I didn't want to be moving around with the diary. Suddenly someone knocked on the door.

"Come in." I kept the diary below my pillow and started playing some game on my phone.

"I heard you are sick so thought of seeing you in person. How are you now?" it was my real father. Whatever I had done a few minutes ago was out of instinct but I was thankful that

I had kept the painting in the closet and diary underneath my pillow.

"I Am feeling much better now." there was an awkward silence but still I was ok with it as I was fuming with anger thinking about him having broken my mother's leg. I didn't feel any sort of attachment towards this man. Although I was trying to but all in vain especially after hearing so much about him.

"Why don't I remember you or mumma?" I didn't know when had I gotten so courageous but I needed to know.

"Those animals injected you with some kind of chemical due to which your memories are washed away. Anyways we are together now and will hopefully create better memories." he was a doting father and I was glad he visited me but now I wasn't in the mood to get all emotional, I wanted to read what was in that diary and as if on cue he got a call.

"I will have to leave now. I will come back tomorrow. Take care." I waved back to him and locked the door.

21 DIARY

I decided to have dinner and start going through the diary at night as I didn't want any further disturbances. Nani and Nana were happy seeing me alright but dreaded the fact that I just had another day to be around them after which I may not be able to visit them as often. I couldn't let them know anything about the diary I had found or every other thing I had come to know about in a day only. I left them to rest and headed to my room. Locking the door and switching off all the lights I proceeded towards the bed and opened the diary.

19th February '93

Dear diary, I sometimes wish I hadn't agreed to this proposal. I wish I wasn't alive.

21st February '93

Dear diary, I am finally getting married. My parents think it's a love marriage but they don't know that I have been forced into this. If I hadn't agreed he had promised to kill my parents in front of me. I know that there isn't any amount of love between us; he is using me for gaining his father's wealth. I am his perfect bait.

Bait??

The first two entries were enough to make me realize that my mother had chosen a diary to convey her feelings instead of a friend or parent. She was already lonely even before it all began

22nd February '93

He didn't feel like asking for it, he just took it from me, made me a woman without my agreement. I don't know how to feel about it as I am his wife, but isn't marriage about two people acting as one soul. I can't even freely write in you anymore. He is coming.

23rd February '93

He has repeated his deeds. He came home drunk late night and slapped me hard as I had fallen asleep. I don't know why he is doing this to me. I wish I was back home.

26th February '93

I have been starved for two days. He has a clinic in the house. I was there monitored by a few doctors. When I dared question him he warned me that if I uttered another single word he would chop of my tongue. After injecting me with numerous different liquids and conducting a hundred different tests I have finally been released. I am still in pain but I need someone to know what I am going through and so I have been pouring my heart out to you.

That man isn't my father. How could he?? With shivering hands I continued turning pages.

29th February '93

He has changed. He took me out for dinner the other day. He even took me to my parents place later although I wasn't allowed to talk to them much but still was happy enough to meet them.

1st march '93

He asked for forgiveness and will be taking me to a party today. I am very happy as finally I can see that love which I have been dying for.

I felt happier reading that he had changed. It wasn't something expected especially after he treated my mother that way. I turned to the next page only to find scribbling. I couldn't make out what exactly was it. After inspecting it for a few minutes I turned to the next page and again found scribbling only. After turning 4–5 more such scribbled pages I finally found another entry which wasn't very easy to understand as the writing was kind of crooked and there were specks of a reddish liquid as well.

8th may '93

He is inhuman. After the party he seemed to be in a good mood and so I decided to ask him why I was kept in that clinic for two days and he simply said I am his lab rat. I am his science experiment and a part of his research and listening to it I had a sudden outburst. I held his collar and at that he slapped me. He became the same monster I was scared of. He thought I was being disrespectful and so he broke all my fingers because I held his collar with those fingers. He wanted me to learn a lesson so that next time I think twice before even touching him. My fingers are still plastered. The servants don't even listen to my pleas. I tried writing in you but it was all in vain. Finally my fingers have gotten better. I wish you could convey my condition to my parents. My fingers are bleeding and so I will have to stop.

20th may '93

I have found out that am pregnant. I don't know how I am supposed to be feeling at this moment.

22nd may '93

Ram found me puking and immediately took me to his clinic. He took my urine samples and soon it was found out that I am actually pregnant. He has been acting differently ever since he found out about it.

2nd august '93

My baby was aborted. The cute little being that was mine was forcibly taken away from me. I feel its absence. They thought I was unconscious but I could hear them saying that my baby has been taken away from me.

He was very caring all the time and mostly around me but I don't really understand why did he do this to me.

4th august '93

He has found out that I write through one of the servants. He has been keeping an eye on me and so I have been more discreet about you. Somehow he has allowed me to paint. I have been provided with the best art supplies still I haven't been allowed to contact my parents. I heard him talking to my parents once. He told them we are vacationing in Jammu and so haven't been able to meet them. I have hidden you behind the little cupboard in the bathroom. I wish to runaway diary, I wish to visit my parents, I wish my baby comes back, I wish I never met Ram, I wish to die.

'Knock knock'

I hid the diary underneath my pillow and turned the small lamp off. Turning the switch on of the lights I headed to open the locked door.

"Am sorry to have disturbed you at this time my child but I just couldn't sl- Were you crying?"

I hadn't realized that I had tears in my eyes. Nani had found me in a vulnerable condition and I didn't know how to react. I was numb. I had an elder sibling who was killed before coming to this life by its own father. My mother was beaten up and raped by that man and I had to go with him if I didn't take any right decisions.

"Something went inside my eyes and I rubbed it a little too harshly so."

"Come with me." she took me the washroom and asked me to wash my eyes with cold water. She kept on telling me how rubbing our eyes can cause damage. I wondered how nani would feel if she would ever come to know the situations her daughter faced.

"You look just like her." she was looking at my face and yet it seemed she wasn't. She missed her daughter and I couldn't do anything about it.

"Nani I will never leave you" hugging her I promised myself, I won't be leaving them.

22 DEEDS

"I forgot to tell you what am I exactly here for, your father had called up, he wants you to stay here for another day as he has some work." she looked so happy while saying it to me although beneath that happiness I could sense that she was scared.

"That's great nani. We can go out for dinner tomorrow." I wanted to spend time with them but currently finding out what happened with mum seemed more important and so I couldn't risk misusing the extra day which was more like a gift.

"Do you have any plans?"

"I might be hanging out with Gautam." I needed his help so why not make him part of my open escapades.

"Is he your boyfriend my dear?" she had that look on her face that suggested 'I know something is going on.'

"NO nani we are just good friends. Now you get back to your room, you might be tired." I wanted to get back to the diary and although I love this old lady I couldn't spend any more time along with her.

"Goodnight my dear." she gave a kiss on my forehead and left.

"Goodnight nani."

I locked the door and turning off the main lights turned on the bedside lamp. Flipping pages I landed on to the next entry.

6th august '93

I was again taken to the clinic yesterday and found out that the only reason my child was taken away from me is because it was a girl. I had tears in my eyes and he just smiled and said 'don't worry we will have a boy next time.' He took away my little girl from me.

I had an elder sister who was killed by that man.

11th September '93

I am officially his slave. He keeps me locked indoors and sometimes don't even lets me use the washroom, I am no more the princess my parents adored. Although since a week he has again started treating me properly. I am scared of him and my life in this house.

15th September '93

I was taken to one of his lavish parties yesterday and he treated me really well. I am feeling happier but I know the worse is coming, I can feel it.

28th October '93

There are no more servants in this house apart from me. I am monitored by a few people but they are not allowed to help me. I clean the entire house which takes up my whole day. I also tried cutting my veins but couldn't as his men came on the right time and took the blade away from me. I was slapped numerous times after that. I am meant to be a lifeless body.

My phone beeped indicating I had received a message. It was from Gautam.

Gautam: Meet me tomorrow morning as early as possible.

Me: Is there something wrong?

Gautam: I can only tell you tomorrow and delete these messages ASAP.

Me: I will meet you at the cafe be there by 8.

I deleted all the texts and didn't get any further replies from him. Gautam never texted, he only called and why did he ask me to delete all those messages. I kept all those thoughts aside and again started reading.

2nd January '94

I can't risk losing you and so I won't be using you anymore.

I flipped pages only to find worn out and torn pages until my eyes landed on a certain page.

7th April '96

Dearest diary,

Writing in you makes me feel like talking to a long lost friend. It's been more than two years now. I have survived several suicide attempts and now am the mother of a very beautiful daughter who turned a year old today. My mother named her Ramika, the perfect combination of her parents. Ram has gotten better by time as he mostly stays in Japan. I feel better here without his presence; I have become friends with my neighbors.' I finally have someone to take care of me. They don't know everything but they know enough. I meet my parents now in every 2–3 months although I never told them about anything as I have learned to adjust. Will have to stop here as my baby girl is crying.

I wish you were here mum. Your baby girl is crying now as well. There were a few torn pages after which I again found a note.

21st June '97

I am again pregnant. I don't know how I am supposed to be feeling anymore. I was sleeping when you started crying in between, he had come home an hour ago and had been sleeping. I didn't wake up immediately so he instead said he will see to you but even after 5 mins you hadn't stopped crying. I woke up to see what was wrong only to find him holding a blade and ready to kill my child. I shrieked and took my child away. My kids are in danger. It's not just me anymore.

He had tried to kill me. The man had tried to kill my mother first and later me.

15th may '98

I have another baby girl. My little Sanika who looks just like her elder sister. Ram doesn't stay with us much anymore. He lives in Japan with his girlfriends. He visits in every two months so that no one finds out about our separation. Life has gotten better apart from the times he visits. We have new neighbors' who have a little boy of Ramika's age. I am happier now.

There were no more entries in the diary but I felt something odd about its cover and when I tore the backside I found a paper stuck up inside.

I hope that it's you my Ramika who has found this diary. I was sure one day you would. I am dying my love. Take care of your sister and stay away from your father. Your father is a mad man. The only reason he decided to marry me was because I was part of his research. He planned on creating the most beautiful and intelligent child. He was the perfect male candidate and I was the perfect other half for his experiment. He killed my first child because he wanted to create a beautiful baby boy and not a girl, later he found out that again I was pregnant with a girl but he couldn't do anything about it so he decided to change the format of his experiment. I don't know what his exact intentions are but you have to stay away my child. Stay away from that man. Be with your neighbors as they know what has to be done. I will miss you my girls. Take care.

My kidnappers are my saviors?? What does mum mean by creating a boy? I need answers and for that I need to find out my fake parents.

Father you will be treated rightly for all your ill deeds.

I fell asleep soon and woke up at the sound of my alarm. Getting ready I headed down to have my breakfast only to find Gautam already having breakfast with nani.

"What are you doing here?"

"Is this the way to greet your guests? Is this what manners you have learnt?" why is nani being so offensive?

"Mrs. Rajput asked me to come over for breakfast yesterday night." I don't know when did nani get his number but I could sense that he was tensed.

I nodded in understanding and began eating, once done we left soon as we knew there is a lot that needs to be talked about.

23 RELATED

"Keep walking and don't utter a single word."

Gautam was securely holding my hand. We had been walking for half an hour now and he still hadn't uttered a word. I could see him relaxing a bit and looking ahead I saw a car. We got inside the car and it started.

"What's wrong Gautam?"

"Everything is fine."

"Mom?? Dad??" it was them, my saviors, my kidnappers. Call them what you want but at this moment seeing them I knew things will be getting better.

Mum hugged me somehow from the front seat whereas dad just held my hand tight and continued driving, at that I gave him a reassuring smile.

"Your aunt called me up yesterday. Your father suspected they are in Gujarat but-"

"But here they are." I was beyond happy but I knew it wasn't over yet. We soon reached at their old abode. We all got down and before I could process anything we were immediately led inside. I had been to my old house but not theirs which looked in a far better condition, as if someone was actually living here all the time.

I hugged them both and they reacted with sobs which I suppose they didn't want me to hear.

"My brave little girl." they both were looking at me with pride in their eyes.

"You have done what we couldn't. I finally don't regret our decision of pretending to be dead." they both were having some sort of eye communication which I couldn't understand but after mum's final nod I knew we are up to something new.

"Sit my love, Gautam you too sit down. Love can you make us all a cup of coffee." Mum nodded her head in agreement and left towards the kitchen.

"Dad I want to know everything. Where were you'll? Why is my real father looking out for you guys-?"

"Calm down. I will tell you everything."

Before I could react the door bell rang. Gautam opened the door and in came him.

"Why is he here?"

It was Lav. Lav Singhania the guy who happens to be my father's alleged adopted son but what was he doing here. He wasn't dressed up like all those times I had seen him instead he was in a loose shirt and low waisted jeans, ruffled hair and smiling. He joined me on the sofa and Gautam pushed him aside and sat beside him. It was odd to see that he and Gautam were having a friendly pushing game.

"Boys!!! Calm down. Ramika he is my son. Our son." mum was the one who gave me shocking news. I could see the resemblance then. He had the similar kind of eyes as dad and that jovial smile as mums. It wasn't really hard to figure out that he was actually their son. Though the kind of way I had seen him dressed up last time made him look like a completely different person. They all were looking at me intently and when Gautam held my hand I snapped out of it.

"We work for the government. Although before we were mere employees in Ram's company but that too was a part of our plan. Ram was always a tricky and cunning man. He had blackmailed your mother into marriage which was something we all knew of. She was rarely brought out in front of the media as well as your grandfather knew something was going on in that house which shouldn't be happening so he started looking around but never found any clues but once somehow he came to know from one of our neighbors' that they had heard her blood curdling scream although Ram would keep on lying to them that either they were out of town or out of the country. Once someone saw Ram carrying a black polythene and dumping it in the nearby dump yard. The person found it very suspicious as Ram would never even get himself a glass of water on his own so throwing a bag of garbage was utterly impossible. He informed your Grandfather about it and he contacted the higher levels as he was a influencive man but nothing could happen as soon Ram left for Japan but he did get the bag found out and what was found in that was unbelievable." in that moment I could see that he was back to a certain phase.

"What was in it?" he was quiet and so were the others and I couldn't keep waiting anymore.

"It was the fetus of your unborn sister. The fetus was in a very bad condition. It was dissected as if someone wanted to see what could be done with It." mum had her head on Lav's shoulder and was slowly weeping, he was trying to calm her. Gautam had his fists clenched but dad and I were the only ones who had no emotions. I had cried enough the other night and I knew that the person who actually happens to be my father deserves to rot in hell. He had killed my sister and my mother so expecting all this from him was obvious. Dad could see that I wanted him to continue further and so he began talking.

"Ram somehow came to know that people have started suspecting him so he started bringing out Anamika to parties and all but there too she wasn't allowed to talk to people, he also started taking her to her parent's house but even there she was never allowed to talk to them alone. Your grandfather knew something was amiss but soon your mum was pregnant with you and there were no more issues between your parents but when your grandparents once visited Anamika they found her with bruises which she clearly said were because of her falling from the stairs. Ram was found to be having numerous affairs in Japan and soon he had divorced your mother after being pressured by the media and Mr.Rajput, but your grandfather knew that Ram wasn't someone who would stop so soon. A week after the divorce it was found that Anamika was again pregnant and so the divorce was kind of nullified as there shouldn't be physical contact but your grandpa knew that Ram had forced Anamika and so he asked for help from a few higher officials and so we were given the job of the safety of you and your mother as well as her unborn child." dad was holding mums hand and I knew they both had done their job well enough. Gautam and Lav left to get lunch for all of us as if on cue mum began talking.

24 DANGER

"Aniket happened to be Ram's school friend and so he knew that Ram wasn't someone easy to be dealt with. We started by applying for the posts of research and development team in Ram's company as we had read in the newspaper that recently they had vacancies and needed new employees so we were soon hired. As I and your dad were college toppers of the biology department it didn't take us too much time to understand the basics and after a few month we both were promoted and although we were already married we always pretended to be just engaged so after a few months Aniket told him that soon we are getting married and need a nice cozy house. He knew that Ram had already started favoring us and so asked us to get shifted in the house besides his." she started eyeing the house and I could see her recalling all those memories.

"We also had a child soon. My little boy Lav and it weren't tough to explain as we were in a live in relationship according to him. Once the house was all furnished we shifted in. We had never met Anamika until one day she landed on our doorstep with Ram and you; she was still heavily pregnant and covered in make up. I am a woman and it wasn't hard for me to see that she was trying to hide a lot of bruises with not just make up but also a huge smile. She immediately took Lav in her hands and started playing with him and you. Soon you'll left but Anamika had also left a little note in Lav's socks.

I and my children's life are in danger. Please help us.

"I still remember when Parul came up to me with that note in her hands. We had thought that Ram was done with his tactics and finally leave them alone but we were wrong so we decided to contact the higher officials but somehow one of them who was close to Ram revealed him about us and also about Anamika's note and before anything could be done he did it."

"He planned everything in advance. He had planned to runaway with little Sanika who was just two days old and you but your mother had sensed things were wrong when she found him holding three passports and a few other documents. So she could only make a call to us. We packed our belongings and kept Lav in the backseat of our car. We waited for Anamika's missed calls. It was her who had told us that she would always inform us of her condition through missed calls but that day we waited and waited only to get a missed call from her and find fire around us. We ran inside to only see Ram fighting with Anamika, in that moment Parul took hold of Sanika who was wailing on the nearby sofa and started looking out for you and I went towards Ram but before I could do anything he had already pushed Anamika in the furnace and pushed me towards the side table and ran away. Parul came soon after and we both left a wailing Anamika. Outside our car wasn't present anymore so we knew that we had lost our son. We left with you two towards Rajput Bhavan and from there on upon your grandfather's advice we got underground."

"Ram had a chopper of one of his friends and he soon left the country. In Japan he wasn't found until a very longtime and so the case was closed. We were happily living with you and Sia after changing yours and our partial identities and shifting from one place to another. It was Rakul's husband who informed us that Ram was coming back to India and probably had found us dead and so we had to pretend our deaths so that he would never come to know about the whereabouts of you two as he would be too busy looking out for the both of us."

"But why didn't nanaji ever tell me anything?" I had that question in my mind since a long time.

"Your nani was never told about all this. Mrs. Rajput would have died of heart attack if she ever found out the kind of cruelty her daughter had faced so she was always kept away from the entire scenario. It is your grandfather and your mother's smartness to be credited for the reason you guys are still alive and so are we. Her one missed call was enough to change the entire plan of your father."

"How did you'll find out Lav?"

"Lav once visited us when we were caught by your father. Looking at him Parul knew that it was Lav but I couldn't believe. She took up some courage and asked him his name, at first he ignored us but later seeing a weeping Parul he gave in and that was enough as Ram out of his foolishness had only changed Lav's surname and when we came to know he was adopted it was more than the needed information and soon we told him he is our son. He left without a word but after a week came back and released us. Ram didn't know about it and with Lav's help we started giving you missed calls. Gautam is Lav's college friend from London, it was a mere co incidence that you two knew him and so with all the help here we are."
I couldn't help but smile along with them. Life had brought upon me havoc but still I had people in life that dearly cared for me although not related to me and on the other hand is my real father who has only caused pain to everyone only for

his selfish motives. The bell rang and I got up to see Gautam and Lav with lots of food bags in their hand. We started eating and talking about here and there when suddenly Lav got a call and after ending it he got back to eating. I could stop myself from spoiling this one peaceful lunch by asking them what I had been dreading to ask since a very long time.

"Why exactly does my father wants me and Sanika to go with him?" everyone stopped eating but Lav still kept dragging his spoon on the entire plate, feeling all eyes upon him he looked up.

"I had a few men going through dad's lab secretly. It was really hard to make out what exactly was his plan but a team of experts were working on it. The call I got now was only to inform me what had they found out."

25 LAB RAT

"What is it Lav?"

"I don't know how am I supposed to explain it?" he kept on unclenching and clenching his fist, it wasn't very easy to make out what Lav could be thinking as he usually had a neutral expression but today and specially now I could see it clearly that he was thinking too much.

I got up from the table and holding his hand I led him to the closest room I could find. Closing the door I didn't knew what to say but at that moment my mind had gotten a mouth of its own.

"Not by blood but still we are related. I know it's a shock for you all this change, meeting your parents and everything but believe me I have been through all this as well and for once I really wish to get rid of all this, especially my father" holding his hand I felt like I was begging him, " Please tell me what's wrong?"

He headed towards the huge balcony which was the only portion of the room that was never used as I could make out my fake parents didn't want anyone prying about their presence." He wants to conduct some experiments upon you and Sanika."

At that moment I recalled finding blood samples, reports and all those stuff in the attic of my old house. But why was all that stuff there and not with my father and are we really his next lab rats.

"I don't know how you are feeling but all I can say is that am sure my parents know something because they have been giving you medicines for a reason I think." he was still looking around and all I could think of was what medicine is he talking about and what is it that the Sharma's have still not talked about. Without wasting any more time I headed to the living room where I found all three of them deeply engrossed in some sort of conversation and on seeing me they all got quiet.

"What more is left to be disclosed?? Please I want to get done with all this, please."

"Sit down." I was too tired to be standing and arguing and so I agreed to my dad and sat on the sofa, Lav too came out of the room and joined Gautam on the other seat. He and dad had some sort of eye communication after which dad looked disappointed.

"We had to tell them someday, then why not today itself." Ma left after saying this.

"After we left with you two, we found out that you both wouldn't respond. Sanika never cried apart from wailing once or twice. Parul knew something was wrong and so we got you two tested. It was found out that you two have been injected with a certain kind of drug that was invented by none other than your grandfather. The drug wasn't disclosed to anyone so it wasn't ever found out what was it made for although we knew that you had lost your memory and so to get it back we started getting you treated with the medicine created by us specifically for your condition. After a year you both were normal but still we were scared and so to avoid any future mayhap we continued giving you the medicine in your food which you never knew off until now. We aren't very sure what exactly Ram's plan is but what we do know is that Anamika knew it and that was the reason she asked us to rescue you. She knew Ram had selfish motives and we are still trying to figure out why he is doing that."

"I and Gautam had been to the attic in your office, what was all that."

"All those were things that were found in your father's lab. He had also collected our son's samples and what not. On further research we found out that he had nails of Anamika's taken off, probably during one of her lab sessions. Whatever we found there was something neither I nor Parul had seen before. He was partially preserving animals which were neither dead nor alive, they were all found in vegetative state and so we started treating them although we couldn't do much. Many of them died and whatever you found there were not even ten percent of the actual slot."

I recalled the state of that squirrel and after hearing that it was found out from my father's lab or it also consisted my mother's nails wasn't a shocker for me. I knew my father has been planning since a long time and if he is back for us it only means that he has been wisely planning it all along although he still isn't aware about Sanika so I am the only lab rat available to him.

"Do you think there is any other way we can find out what he has been planning for me?"

"Tonight he has called me up for documentation and other purposes. He plans on shutting down his entire process unit here in India and shift his entire base to Japan. He thinks that am with Gautam whenever am not in the house although he isn't aware that I have set up a little camera in my bedroom and soon after which I found out that he had been collecting my hairs and various things from my bedroom. Going through one such recording I found out that he was also accompanied by a team of scientists who only talk to him and can't communicate with anyone else but I befriended one of them's daughter back in Japan who happens to be of Indian origin and she is the one who has been helping me find out a lot of things, she is in India and will be there with us tonight and hopefully with her help I might be able to get what we all have been looking for."

"Lav don't put yourself in danger, don't do anything foolish." I had that elder sister instincts towards Lav the way I had for Sia and Tara and I knew tonight will be something that we all will be awaiting for.

Soon after I and Gautam headed to the Rajput bhavan and Lav headed to meet my father. I decided to meet The Katyal's and then head towards our house after meeting them and complaining to them about Gautam at which they would yell at him I decided to take my leave , Gautam dropped me on my doorstep, he was about to leave when ," Why are there so many cars in the driveway?"

I looked behind me to notice 3 huge cars and then holding his hand I ran towards the house, I noticed a lot of security guards and body guards guarding my house. Heading inside I heard the noise of a lot of people and hearing one particular voice I knew that bringing along Gautam was definitely a good idea as I was going to be needing a lot of support tonight.

In the dining room were my grandparents, Lav and the girl he had been talking about along with a few more people which could probably be the team of scientists and there sitting in the center most chair was my father.

26 MALE

"And here comes my lovely daughter." my father had gotten up from his chair and was gesturing me to join him, to people he would look like a very loving and caring father but I could see that behind all that love and affection was hatred, anger and hollowness. His motives had not only killed my mother but also his soul.

"Go" Gautam was pulling me towards my father as he could make out that I didn't feel like going near that man. Hugging him was an all together different thing. I looked around and could see a look of helplessness in my grandparent's and Lav's eyes.

"Mary, this is my lovely child, Ramika." Mary was one of the few scientists present, she just nodded and continued eating, I sat beside Gautam and began having dinner. I knew something was amiss and so when Lav got up to use the washroom I on cue excused me from the dinner and left to join him. I followed him only to be on call.

"Yes he is here; I don't know what to do. Dad please do something before he gets away with Rhea." I knew he was talking to my dad. I could see fear in Lav's eyes. He immediately ended the call.

"I knew you would follow, the only way we can find out what he wants is by getting our hands on his briefcase and one of those scientists. My friend can't help me anymore but I think Mary can. You have to find Mary immediately and with Gautam's help bring her to the outhouse."

“But how will I do that in front of everyone.” before my statement ended the lights were out.

“It’s part of the plan, now go and find Mary and Gautam.”

I ran towards the living room, although the lights were out it seemed as if I didn’t need the lights anymore. I found Gautam in the corridor with a partially conscious Mary. We took her to the outhouse and found Lav arriving with his friend soon after us.

“What will we do when people find her missing?”

“Her clone is in the dining room with others as well as our clones. Lights won’t be back for another 25 minutes and your dad won’t create havoc as he himself is not in proper senses due to a dose of one of his own medicines which he has created for instant fainting which Lav gave him. The electricity supply has been cut for the entire area so we are safe.” Gautam finished explaining and all I could do was stare at him in awe. I knew he and Lav were smart but all this was just something else.

Soon Mary was in her senses and before she could yell Lav held her hands and started talking to her in Japanese, I couldn’t understand a word of it and so the entire 10 minute conversation was a little irritating for me and Gautam.

“Male, yes male.” she said that statement in a pure accented English after which Lav wouldn’t utter another word.

“Time is up. We need to get her back.” upon those words uttered by Gautam Lav came back to his senses and injected Mary with something and soon we were all in the dining room just minutes before the power supply was back.

My dad looked pale and Mary was now back to normal.

"I don't feel too well so we will be resting here for a few hours and by 4 am we will leave for Japan." he didn't utter another single word and without even asking any sort of permission from my grandparents he left to one of the rooms upstairs accompanied by two of his bodyguards. Soon all left to the guestrooms guided by nani and eventually the only people left were me, Gautam, Lav and his friend. I asked them all to accompany me to my mum's room.

"Lav what is he trying to do with me?" Lav had been sitting quietly in one corner since the time we had arrived in the bedroom. Gautam had fallen asleep and Lav's friend was busy on Skype with someone.

"He is trying to create a perfect male specie."

"What do you mean Lav?"

"It's you whom he is trying to convert into a perfect male specie."

Until now I only knew of death as the worst scenario, but someone trying to snatch away your loved ones, then your gender and identity. Was I such a huge shame for him that he was trying to change my gender? I couldn't help myself from letting fall a few lose tears.

"It's not just you."

"What do you mean, does he know about Sia?"

"I am the second half of his experiment." I couldn't comprehend what Lav was trying to say. At one point I was happy to know that he hadn't come to know about Sia and at another point I was more scared to know that it just wasn't me who was in danger but also Lav.

"Your father is trying to interchange genders." it was Lav's friend who had gotten up from her old position and was now sitting beside Lav holding his hand.

"He intends on interchanging your and Lav's genders." I could see fear on her and Lav's face and for once I knew what I had to do.

"Lav can I have your cell phone." it was Gautam who was now completely awake. Lav handed him his cell phone.

"Hello, dad? Yes it's me." Gautam went towards a corner and kept talking for a few minutes, Lav on the other hand looked even more shocked and I couldn't make out what was going on now.

"He is coming."

"Who is coming?"

"Gautam are you sure you want to involve him?" Lav looked relieved and scared.

"May I know what the hell is going on?" I was beyond frustrated by these secrets in my life and I couldn't handle anymore.

"Gautam's dad is coming here."

"Rhea I never got the time to tell you, apparently my dad is the head of the Indian intelligence department. I am sorry for not telling you before but now the situation is way severe and I know he is the only person who can handle everything."

"We couldn't involve him as he works for an entire nation and is usually on secret missions so it is very hard to contact him but what that person is trying to do has begun in our country and the drugs have also been created here as well as the experiment is highly dangerous and so involving him was perfect for now."

"It's alright Gautam; I just don't understand why does my own father want to do this to Me.?" I was relieved true but I was also scared, what if Gautam's father doesn't arrive on time. God why make life so scary that every living second turns out to be a nightmare.

27 MANIAC

Everyone had fallen asleep, except me. I knew that we could be safe if Gautam's father arrives on time but what if he doesn't? Life had turned out to be a jigsaw puzzle for me. A puzzle with no end. The pieces were too different to have a link but something seemed to be missing.

I started recalling everything that had happened in these two years. Everything seemed surreal but I knew there had to be some reason for my father's doings. He was a genius and genius doesn't turn into maniacs for no reason. I knew I would regret my actions later but I had to do what I was planning to. Typing a message of,

"If its past 2 am and am not in room come to find me. I had been to my father's room."

I sent this message to both Gautam and Lav so that whomsoever woke up and found me missing would at least know where they could start finding me from. I left towards the room where I had last seen him last heading off to.

"We need to leave by 3am as the department is planning to attack by 4. Remember we don't have to wake them up, just get hold of Lav and Ria. Inject them with the anti-reactive anesthetic as that will keep them unconscious for a longer period of time." I knew that there was someone who had been updating him about our moves, everything that we had been planning for was somehow known by him but now that I was here there was no looking back and so I headed inside.

There were four of his bodyguards and two of his scientists who were present there along with him and on seeing me none of them seemed shocked which was weird.

"I knew you would arrive sooner or later, come sit." I sat down on the chair opposite to his.

"I would like each one of you'll to leave this room and make sure that no one comes inside and by no one I hope you understand whom am I emphasizing on." everyone left after his malice filled voice ordered them to get out in the most indirect way possible. It wasn't tough to make out that by no one he meant Lav and Gautam.

"Come, I need to show you something." He shifted a painting on the wall behind which I could see a passage.

"Don't be scared, I am your father. You are the only family to me now and I don't intend on losing you by any chance so don't worry, you are in safe hands." I had no choice but to follow him through that passage but what I saw later was the actual shocking part.

"Your mother had told me once about this secret passage, who knew her information would come so handy to me someday. Sit down, I won't eat you up." the passage led us to my mother's room. It was fishy that why would mum reveal such an information to this man out of all the people she could have relied on.

"I loved your mother more than she could have ever asked for, but she couldn't give me a son. I didn't ever ask for anything else from her apart from a perfect son who would in future inherit all this that happens to be mine today." He turned around to look at me but he wasn't really looking at me. He seemed to be deep in thought when anger flashed in his eyes.

"You were not supposed to be born but still here you are great in health, as pretty as your mother, alive and a girl" it was hatred, the only emotion that I could have sensed in his voice.

"My little girl, don't cry. You see the reason why I never wanted girls was because the only thing they ever did was cry and demand." I didn't realize when had I started crying but even before I could wipe my tears he was already holding me by my neck. His fingernails had started digging deep into my flesh, I was not able to breathe anymore and it was getting hazy in front of my eyes. For a moment there I had started praying to god to take me away from this hell hole, it was getting more difficult for me to even keep my brain working. Closing my eyes I started awaiting my end.

"Don't be so relieved, I won't let you die now. After all I have found the way to make my dreams come true. You will be the perfect male and when I will sell you to further nations for research purposes you will get me lots of money." He left me to choke upon my own saliva and kept on talking and laughing. I started looking out for ways I could let Lav or Gautam know that I wasn't in the room they could had been trying to get in and at that moment it striked me that I just somehow had to get my hands on my cell phone as just by pressing the number three on my dial pad I could let them know of my location.

"Didn't you ever love me?" I had to get his attention away from me and for that I had to keep him involved in his talks and what better than his favorite topic.

"I love science and money and once you are of use to me I will start loving you too." turning away he looked towards my mother's portrait and at that moment I did what I had to and kept my phone back in my pocket, I was just hoping that they notice it before it's too late.

"Your mother wasn't a bad woman either; it's just that she was too nosy and never agreed on using you or Sia for my experiments. The day I decided to kill her was something I wasn't planning for but I knew that someone had to die so why not her." he was now scribbling on my mother's portrait and I didn't want to see what was he doing with it but then I saw blood dripping and when I looked further I saw that he had cut his palm in the process of ruining my mother's picture. The once beautiful picture now had my father's blood drops right below her eyes which made it seem like she had been shedding tears of blood. He turned around and headed towards me with that blade in his hand.

"Why don't we start the process now itself?"

"Your eyes are just like hers so we will have to change the color of your lenses" he made a cross like mark right below my eyes with his blade, I didn't know what to do apart from waiting for my saviors and so I decided on being still as I knew that no reactions would lessen his pleasure.

"Your eyebrows will also have to be more bushy, thicker lips, a better nose, strong jaw line" he kept going on and kept marking all my face with criss cross markings. I had started feeling dizzier as some of his cuts were deep enough due to which I had been bleeding more than needed and right before he could make another cut I started falling into blackness and that's when I heard Gautam yelling my name.

All I wanted to do was sleep. I was finally away from him. Sia was safe and hopefully Gautam and Lav won't let that man getaway from all his nasty crimes. I could finally rest and be at peace.

28 LOST AND FOUND

All I could feel was numbness, for a second I felt happier to have finally gotten away from him but then I heard it. I could hear 3-4 people discussing something, it was tough to make out whether I was dreaming or my mind was playing games with me, at that moment I felt a prick on my head, I could feel a certain cool liquid being injected in my head. After trying very hard I was finally able to convince myself that I wasn't dead yet, maybe I had a few more dreaded years on this planet. I was still trying to gain complete consciousness when I heard him,

"I know you are awake, you don't need to act anymore. The liquid was specially injected so that you gain complete consciousness; I need you to see how I change you from filthy worthless women to a worthy male. I want you to feel the change and I want you to feel the pain." I knew he was standing mere inches away from my face, he had spitted on my face to make me realize that I was actually filthy to him. Soon someone called him and I could feel him leaving.

I immediately opened my eyes only to find a completely white room but when had I gotten here? Was I already in Japan? Had he gotten away with me and if yes what happened to Lav and Gautam. While thoughts kept my mind busy, my eyes started in taking the scenario in front of me.

I was lying on a hospital bed with fluids attached to my body; I had certain markings made on my neck and hands which looked like markings made prior to surgeries. There was a glass door outside which I could see people gathering instruments like scissors, blades and lots of other surgical items. I tried looking for my cell phone and realized that I wasn't in my previous clothing anymore, I was in a hospital gown which was too huge for me yet covered me completely although when I tried getting up I found my feet locked up to the bed in a cuff like thing.

"So you seem ready and eager for this procedure, well it has already begun, as you can see that these tubes attached to you have already started doing the internal change, these will give a boost to your hormones and don't worry as no one will find us here." He started changing the tubes when I knew that I had to know where I was, I need to try once.

"Where are we?" With the end of my question came a throbbing and painful slap on my face which had busted my lip.

"You address me as SIR from now on; I don't like manner less people anywhere in my vicinity. See cause of your low grade behavior you had to get such a pretty face scarred." he started wiping the blood from my lip and that's when I saw her enter.

"Hi" it was Lav's friend, the same girl who pretended on being determined to help us and that's when it striked me that she had been the informer all the time. She was the missing piece.

"I hope you have met Kamiro before, she happens to be one of my most prized possessions and also your step mother." he kissed her in front of my eyes, this man never deserved my mother and this deceiving women is definitely perfect for him. Although him being with her for the sole purpose of love is something highly unbelievable.

"Let's begin love." I knew Kamiro was enjoying all this. She seemed more eager and excited than him.

I started thinking of different ways to postponed his work and then,

"I would like to use the washroom for one last time, Sir." I said in the most possible lady like manner with my head bent down.

"Kamiro accompany her to the washroom, although its not really needed as there is no way of getting away from me." once I was inside the washroom I pretended to act as if I was really doing what I had to and started looking out for anything that could be handy at the moment. My legs and hands were cuffed but being lanky enough upon some pushing I knew I could remove the cuffs from my hands. I was still thinking when the lights went off.

I immediately headed to the washroom door and locked it with my cuffs using my hair pin. It was pitch black and I could hear my father yelling upon everyone as well as asking Kamiro to get me out. I looked around but couldn't see anything so I started feeling things with my hands and that's when I found a cabinet; I opened it up and got inside, shutting the cabinet properly. I was still trying to fit in when I heard a beep and after which the surface below me started moving, I got in hysterics thinking that maybe I will be found again.

I heard another beep after which the door in front of my face opened up. I looked around and found a window that was too properly closed by thick glass panes. I looked out and understood where I was.

I was in my old abode. I was where it all began and it didn't take me long to realize that I was in my mother's room. With the help of the moon light I locked the doors and waited for consequences to happen. I waited and waited but instead of anyone's arrival I felt dizziness coming back to me.

I woke up to see smoke around me but it wasn't the smoke cause of which I had woken up, it was someone's voice, someone was calling out to me. I wanted to yell back to them and let them know where I was but the smoke had gotten to my lungs, it was getting more and more difficult for me to breathe and so mustering up all my energy before I could lose myself I yelled back,

"I am here"

I felt someone holding my hands; I opened my eyes to see Gautam holding my hands deep in sleep. I was in a hospital bed an actual one this time. In the far end was Lav sleeping on a sofa with his head on his mother's lap.

I started coughing and that's how everyone instantly noticed that I was up.

"Finally after two days you felt like waking up and that too you do by disturbing everyone else." Gautam immediately left my hand; although he was trying to act like a jerk again I could see that he was more than relieved to see me awake.

"Says the one who didn't leave her side even for a complete minute." I couldn't help but laugh at Lav's sarcastic comment. Gautam just snorted and left the room and Lav soon followed him.

A nurse came in a while later and told everyone that I was in a much better state of health and could go back home in two days. When she left I was left alone with my fake mum. She was caressing my forehead and asked her what I had been waiting to do,

"What happened?"

"Gautam and Lav got frantic when they couldn't find you anywhere, you weren't in your father's room. Apparently no one was there in that house. Everyone had left. Gautam straight headed to our old house and his father who had arrived by then got security sped up on airports, stations and highways. Lav headed to us, we were thinking upon what to do when we received a miss call at first we didn't think of it as anything but soon there were 4 more. We don't know who gave those missed calls as it was on our old landline but we knew it was a sign. We called up Gautam's father who reached up on time. We entered inside only to find the house set up on flames. It was Gautam who ran upstairs to look out for you and got you down in time as the house was catching fire too soon.'

"What about everyone else?"

"We couldn't find him, we caught everyone else but he was never found."

Hearing about him still being alive only got me more furious.

"We couldn't find who gave those missed calls, but it was like déjà vu. We were scared that we might lose you just like how we lost your mother years ago but faith was in your favor. Gautam was somehow sure that he would find you and so he did. Unfortunately you or anyone of us isn't safe anymore and so we will be leaving this country soon. With the help of Gautam's father we will get a new identity and a better life."

"Do you mind Aunt if I talk to her for a while."

"Sure Gautam"

"He is a good guy; don't lose him." aunt left saying those words in my ears." *I know you will be leaving soon. I also know a lot has happened with you. That day when I reached upon the door to your mother's room, finding you in that state only made me realize that I can never see you in pain. I will do my best to find your father and make him*

and Kamiro rot in hell only if you say yes to me." Gautam was now on his knees in front of my bed, *"Will you marry me?"*

I didn't know how I was supposed to react to this marriage proposal.

"Look don't say no, I have never proposed anyone like this and even if you want to don't tell anyone else about it but please try saying yes."

I was still thinking when I saw everyone enter the door and yell,

"Say yes"

"Yes."

EPILOGUE

It's been two days since I haven't received any calls from Gautam. I know he isn't a kid and I shouldn't be fussing over it but can't help it.

"Chillax. He is in the mountains, you barely get food there so having nearly no network is a very high possibility. He will call back as and when he gets free so stop worrying and focus on your exam preparations." Lav has changed a lot after what happened two years back. He left the house once he was done messing with my hairs as well as my mind.

Well yes, I did say yes to Gautam but no we didn't marry, instead we got engaged as he still had to get settled and I had to complete my studies as well. We aren't Rhea or Lav anymore and we are in one of the busiest cities in the world where in the midst of hustle and bustle that man won't be able to ever find us. Mum and Dad have gotten back to their detective work and are doing well enough. Lav is also a student in the same university as I am although he too plans on being a detective just like mum and dad where as I still prefer being a psychiatrist. Sia, Rakul aunt and every else too got a complete change of identification and are currently on a World Tour with my Uncle.

Soon after I get rid of my exams we will be planning for our marriage that's what Gautam had promised me but I think he is happier being in the woods, camping with his pals rather than planning about his own marriage.

I was done with my revisions and so after getting all the luck from my parents I left to appear for my last examination. Mornings happen to be the rush hour of this city so it's not really easy to walk faster when you already have nearly hundreds of people ahead of you trying to do the same thing.

After too much trouble I finally reached the subway wherein I was so engrossed in my own thoughts that I not even once thought that I might bump into someone, well it was his mistake as well but men, they never accept it. I fell with a loud thud which got my books out of my bag and also made me wince in pain because of the impact the fall had on my bums. No it's not at all funny.

I started blabbering about not seeing and all and started packing my bag, the man too helped me assemble my stuff and before I could even look at him, he left. Something oddly seemed familiar about him and the only person I could think of was the man who used to get me those letters, but that man was Lav so it couldn't be him.

"Romeo takes me somewhere we can be alone." I hated this song ever since Gautam had set it up as my ringtone for his calls. Relief flashed over me when I released finally that jerk had called up.

"I am so so so sorry. We went fishing and I by mistakenly ended up dropping my cell phone in the river and others didn't have enough battery in their phones so I had to wait until my phone completely dried up. How are you my baby?"

"I thought you completely forgot that you have a fiancé. Come back soon alright. I am nearly done with my exams and I don't intend on wasting my time by worrying about your whereabouts. Take care of yourself and keep missing me."

"Gautam?? You there?"

"I am fine; you just take care of yourself. I got a video message from my father and according to him your father is back in town. So be safe until I get there. Love you."

"Love you."

I didn't let my mind wander towards what Gautam had said as I wanted to focus on my exams for the time being. Once I was done I started stuffing stuff from my locker in my bag when I found an envelope.

The same kind of envelope.

I immediately left to my house taking a cab.

"Mum, Dad, Lav please come here."

"What's wrong?"

I showed them the envelope. We all sat down and then I opened it up. Inside were the pictures of my grandparents. Lying in a pool of blood. With the similar kind of hatches he had made on my face years back, their nails removed. Although we all were shedding tears I knew they were at peace as they had to give up a lot in order to change their identities and shift to a peaceful holy city of India. There were no letters but when I turned the pictures, there it was, written in blood.

"You are next"

THE END OR THE BEGINNING…